The Summer-House Loon

Blind Professor Muffet, his favourite student Ned (the 'Loon'), his beautiful secretary, Caroline and his bumbling guide-dog, Mandy, give Ione a riotous introduction to the problems of adult life – how *not* to cope with love, money, careers, loneliness, drink and forty uninvited guests coming to tea.

The Summer-House Loon

ANNE FINE

MAMMOTH

First published in Great Britain 1978
by Methuen Children's Books Ltd
Magnet edition published 1979
Reprinted 1985
Published 1990 by Teens
Reissued 1992 by Mammoth
an imprint of Mandarin Paperbacks
Michelin House, 81 Fulham Road, London SW3 6RB

Mandarin is an imprint of Reed Consumer Books Ltd

Text copyright © 1978 Anne Fine

A CIP catalogue record for this title
is available from the British Library

ISBN 0 7497 0184 6

Printed in Great Britain
by Cox & Wyman Ltd, Reading

For my mother and father

1

Ione sat, cross-legged, on the summer-house floor, tracing patterns with her fingertips on the cool grey flagstones. She was thinking about resolutions – her summer holiday resolutions, which she was just about to make.

The summer-house was right at the far, tangly end of the garden, way away across the lawn from the house. It was octagonal and tall, like an over-starched tea cosy. Its sides were latticed, made of thin strips of wood nailed across one another, diagonally. They were not glassed, so they let in the sun or the wind or the rain.

On this particular evening, though, it was warm, without even a breeze; and the rays of the sinking sun gleamed steadily through the diamond-shaped holes, reflecting them again, but pink this time, upon the pitted stone floor. The shapes reflected furthest from Ione, near the sun's side, were squat and close, like honeycomb; but those where she sat, dead in the centre of the summer-house, under the glassed-over top which supported the rusting weather vane, were long and elegant diamonds, more like arrows pointing both ways.

'Lozenges,' Ione said to herself. 'Like lozenges.'

She always found great difficulty in making resolutions of any sort, even though she did it so often. Firstly, she found it hard to keep her mind upon the subject; and secondly, she never knew how high a standard she wished to set for herself. After all, she did not wish to be perfectly perfect.

She remembered that at the beginning of last term she had resolved three things, and she counted them off again, and thought about them.

The first had been to do her homework on the night that it was given, neatly and well. This resolution had lasted almost until half-term. After that, she had had to renew it about every second Monday morning until the last week of the term, when she hadn't bothered, since nothing mattered except the dancing display and the swimming competition.

The second resolution had divided into two halves: not to tease the biology teacher, who was called Miss Smith; and not to tease her father's guide dog, who was called Mandy.

It was, she soon found, easy enough not to tease Mandy. Ione had only fallen into the habit through boredom, in any case; and once the first few days of ignoring Mandy were over, Ione had decided that the old dog was more of a bore herself than the boredom that had led Ione into teasing her in the first place.

It had been a lot harder, at the start, not to tease Miss Smith. But then, during only the second week of the term, Miss Smith had squashed Ione flat by suggesting haughtily that perhaps the rest of the class found Ione's persistent comments and feeble jokes as irritating and unamusing as she herself did. Ione could still remember how scarlet she had gone, and how everyone, even her closest friends, had giggled at her so meanly. She had been cold and reserved in biology from that moment on; and until the end of the term she never once put up her hand, even when she was sure that she knew the right answer, and no one else did.

So that resolution had, in a sense, been kept *for* her as well as *by* her; but at least it had been kept.

The last resolution had been to read to her father whenever she knew that he really wanted her to.

Ione's father was blind. He was a University Professor, who also wrote history books and articles. Mounds of papers came for him in every post, and his study was piled high with thick, heavy files, covered in brown wrapping-paper. These he could read for himself, using his fingertips. The papers were written in braille, and his fingers ran over the little dots punched in patterns on the paper almost as quickly as Ione herself could read normal black printed alphabet letters with her eyes.

He kept, in his study at home, an enormous green tape-recorder, as well as a little machine he could carry around with him that had several levers and made a tic-tac noise, pushing out long streams of thin, white paper, rather like the end of a bus-conductor's ticket reel, and a huge, solid kind of typewriter that had to stay in one place and that punched those odd, holey lumps of braille into the paper instead of printing letters.

And he had a secretary, Miss Hope, from the Agency, who came most days to transcribe, or put it all into normal printing on her own, smaller, type-writer. Then other historians, who weren't blind, and therefore could not follow braille, could read the books and articles Ione's father wrote.

Miss Hope was tall and thin, and not very depend-able. Her mother was blind, which was why, although she was sighted herself, she had once learned braille. Miss Hope was trying to teach Ione braille, too; but with all her schoolwork, Ione did not seem to have much time, and wasn't getting on too well.

So with all this equipment, although you couldn't really call Miss Hope equipment, Ione's father managed very well. But whenever any of the import-ant history journals arrived in the early morning post, Professor Muffet would ask Ione, over break-fast, to read out the titles of the articles that were in them that month. And if any of them were about Sardinia, or Early Trade Routes, then he would twist about excitedly on his chair, wafting toast crumbs all over the carpet and Mandy, and he would say to Ione, as casually as he could manage, 'Perhaps Miss Hope will find time . . . but if you're not doing anything until the bus comes . . . perhaps just a paragraph?' Then he would trail off, waiting hopefully for her to reply.

And mostly she did read at least a couple of paragraphs out for him, before it was time to rush off to catch the bus; although each paragraph was almost always nearly a page long, and what little she understood of it seemed awfully boring.

But sometimes she got up from the breakfast table in a hurry, and said she had promised to meet Josephine early at the bus-stop, or she had forgotten to feed Mandy yet, or she had some homework to finish before she left.

Then he would smile at her, and say, 'Oh, well. It can wait. I don't mind. You rush off.'

But she knew that he did mind really, because sometimes Miss Hope was awfully late, and sometimes she even phoned to say she couldn't come at all. So Professor Muffet had to sit all day, wondering what the article on his table that he so much wanted to read, said.

And so she had made that her third resolution. Had she kept that one? She thought she had done much better than ever before. But she had sometimes told the same old lies to escape, so that was only a half-keep really.

So. Three resolutions, and what was the score? One just over half; one almost completely; one better than ever before, but still not good enough to stop her feeling guilty. You could, if you were generous with yourself, call it three passes; but Ione had her doubts.

She ran her finger round and round a pink diamond, still thinking hard. The sun had sunk almost into the hedge by now, and though the diamonds were getting longer and longer, their pink was fading fast. But still she sat and thought.

Ione wondered if there was any real *point* in making all these resolutions. Perhaps she would have behaved in just the same way, all last term, whether she had made them or not. Perhaps there was no point in going to any trouble making new ones for these summer holidays. Perhaps she should just try drifting through, day by day, and seeing what happened. She wondered if that was what other people did.

Maybe she was the only person in the world who ever made resolutions, except on New Year's Eve, when everybody made them – even her father. It would be nice to know where she stood about this. It would be good if there were someone she could ask.

Ione did not often wish that she still had a mother. But that summer evening, as the hedge ate up the last splodge of sun, and the last pink diamond on the summer-house floor shrank neatly into itself and disappeared, she wished for all the world that she still did.

She said aloud, without realising that she was saying it aloud, 'Maybe I am the only person in the world who wants to be different from what I am.'

2

'I doubt that.'

A deep, pleasant voice sounded right behind Ione.

'Indeed, I know for a fact that it's not the case. I, too, think the same quite often.' The voice broke off for a second's thought, and then added, 'Though I don't think it in quite the same way as you do, grammatically.'

Ione had swung round, astonished, when she first heard the strange voice. Now she was staring, wide-eyed, at the interloper. The interloper stared steadily back at her.

He saw a slim, small girl with shredded-looking straight brown hair and a fringe that fell over her eyes. She was wearing a flapping blue shirt which was far too big for her, and a darker blue pair of jeans. He could not make out the colour of her eyes, although he tried, because of the fringe. Her jeans, he noticed, were streaked with slimy-looking grass stains on both knees, as though she had been kneeling on the edge of a damp lawn, weeding flower beds. He had no idea at all how old she was.

She saw, in spite of her fringe, the tallest young man she could have imagined, leaning against the rickety wooden doorpost behind her, his grave, long face half in shadow. She thought he must be at least twenty years old, for he had a longish, drooping, cowboy moustache, and she couldn't imagine anyone younger than twenty years old daring to wear one. The moustache was slightly lighter in colour than his hair, which was browner than Ione's, and only a little bit shorter. He was thin, and dressed, like her, in blue jeans. His shirt was a very grubby white colour. Round his neck straggled a tie of several very violent colours, and a bottle-green corduroy jacket dangled from his fingers down behind his back, collecting dust and cobwebs off the doorpost.

He looked as though he had been leaning there, inside the summer-house, for hours.

'You eavesdropped,' she accused him, hot with embarrassment. 'You were listening to every single word I said.'

'True,' he said. 'Though you only said one thing, apart from "lozenges", which didn't really count. I can't *think* what you've been thinking about, all this while.'

He stared around the summer-house. In one of its eight corners was spread the tattered remains of an ancient spider's web. The spider was long since gone, but the web was enormous. He smiled at it in admiration. Then he turned back to Ione, still smiling in admiration. 'You must be a great thinker,' he told her. 'Sitting so still for so long. Anyone else would have gone home for tea *ages* ago.'

'Why haven't you, then?' she countered. 'And what are you doing in our garden?' She finished up fiercely, 'Who *are* you?'

The moment she had said it, she realised how much she must have sounded to him like the snooty Caterpillar in *Alice in Wonderland*. Like the Caterpillar who sat on the flat mushroom, smoking his hookah and asking Alice in such a haughty, off-putting way, 'Who are *you*?'

And the moment after that she realised that he, too, was thinking exactly the same thing. For she saw his long, serious face begin to crumple into another of its smiles. Then, to her great relief, before the smile fully happened, he set his face solemnly again.

And from that moment on, because he had not teased her when he could have done, and clearly would have liked to, she liked him hugely and forever.

'But what are you doing in our summer-house?' she persisted.

'I am trespassing,' he said simply, and pulled thoughtfully at his droopy moustache.

Ione did not know what to say. Neither did he. So they stared at one another for a little while longer.

Then the interloper began to wriggle untidily into

his jacket, as though he were about to leave. Ione suddenly knew two things, both at the same time. She knew that he was *too* thin, probably from not eating properly and regularly; and she knew that he was very unhappy about something.

So she spoke to him again, out of kindness. And at that very moment he spoke to her again, out of curiosity.

'What is your name?' she asked him.

'What *were* you thinking about?' he asked her.

He answered first. His was, after all, much the easier question to answer.

'My name is Ned Hump,' he told her.

She admired the way he said it, so straightforward and unapologetically. And his name was almost as bad as hers. Ione was always most embarrassed when she had to say her own name to people, especially to total strangers. She usually mumbled it out so mangled the first time that she had to go through all the agony again.

She decided to be equally forthright with him.

'I was wishing that I had a mother again,' Ione said. She added defensively, 'I don't wish it very often, but sometimes I do.'

Ned Hump stared at her gravely for a long, long while. Then he said, 'It works both ways, you know. It works exactly the same way backwards, if that makes it any better for you. People who *do* have mothers sometimes wish they hadn't. They don't wish it very often, either; but sometimes they do.'

It did make it better for her. It made it a whole lot better. She felt very grateful to him.

Meanwhile, he had fallen into another of his long, moustache-tugging silences. Ione was already beginning to get used to them. So while he gazed moodily over her head, as if she were not there at all, and out through the summer-house lattice-work, towards the lawn and the house beyond, she counted the spangles and the circles on his tie.

There were twice as many pink spangles as there were orange circles on the tie, except for at the bottom, where the circles seemed to be fraying faster than the spangles. She wondered who on earth had given it to him. It was not the sort of tie an aunt would buy. The colours looked even more violent now, clashing against the bottle-green jacket that he had put on again. She could only suppose that he had bought the tie himself.

She wondered if he trespassed often in her garden, or if this were the first time. She wondered if he might be dangerous. He was certainly a little odd. She thought again how he was far too thin.

She wondered if she dare invite him in for tea, since he looked so hungry. Perhaps he was one of her father's students, and had a dreadfully mean landlady who gave him meals that were not nourishing enough for someone of his height. He was very tall, and looked as though he ought to eat a lot.

At last, at long last, he broke his own silence.

'I, too, have my problems,' he told her.

He let his knees buckle up beneath him and his body fold up like an old-fashioned clothes horse, until he was sitting on the floor at her side.

'I am in love with Caroline,' he said, tragically.

'Caroline?'

'Caroline Hope,' he explained, irritably. Then he added, just as irritably Ione thought, 'I adore her.'

'Miss Hope,' said Ione, comprehending at last.

'You know her?' he asked. 'Of course you do. You live here. She works here.' Light was dawning, visibly, on his face. 'You must be Professor Muffet's daughter.' He thought about this. 'If he has one, that is,' he felt obliged to add. 'And that is how you know Miss Hope,' he concluded, triumphantly.

'She types for Daddy,' Ione explained. 'From braille. It's called transcribing. She does it from the tape-recorder, or from his paper reels of braille. Or even just while he stands over her and dictates it all.' She noticed that the stranger was, once again, staring over her head, and out through the summer-house lattice-work. She thought perhaps it was because he was not understanding.

'To transcribe means to copy out in normal writing, or on a typewriter,' she told him. 'Perhaps you didn't know that?'

'I did,' he said. His attention was recalled. Then, seeing her face drop – for she felt foolish – he added quickly: 'But purely by chance. I met the word in a book only a few weeks ago.'

Ione smiled at him. He had tact. It occurred to her

that she might make tact her *only* summer holiday resolution.

And once this decision had been made, she felt as though a weight had been lifted from her mind. She felt carefree. She smiled at him again, even more warmly. It was the second thing he had made her feel better about, already.

But he did not seem to notice her pleasure. His eyes were straying again.

'Miss Hope refuses to marry me,' Ned Hump was continuing with his explanation of his problems. 'She refuses frequently and point-blank. I am forever proposing her. I propose all but daily. And she is forever being nasty to me in return. She is nasty to me whenever she gets the chance. Which is at least once a day.'

'Perhaps she gets bored with all your proposals?'

'I think not,' said Ned Hump. 'After all, if she were bored, she need only accept my offer once, and the whole repetitive process could come to a timely end. I should never have to ask her again.'

'Unless you divorced,' said Ione.

Ned Hump stared at Ione, trying to digest this observation. Then he said, politely, 'Quite.'

'Perhaps she wants to marry someone else,' suggested Ione, trying to be a little more practical. 'My father, for example. She's always nice enough to him.'

'I think not,' said Ned Hump again. 'Much as I respect your father and his work – though, Lord knows, I disagree with every single word he says about the Early Sardinian Trade Routes – I do not think that Caroline Hope would wish to marry him. Or, if she did, it would be from sheer contrariness on her part. She is in love with *me*.'

'If she loved you, she would marry you,' Ione pointed out, still trying to be practical.

'There are certain aspects of the warped character of Miss Caroline Hope that have clearly escaped you up until now,' Ned Hump told Ione. 'For one thing, the lady has Notions. She has Notions about Roofs Over Heads, and Good Starts In Life, and Little Somethings Put Away In Case Of Rainy Days, and so on and so forth. She is full of Notions. Chock-a-block full.'

He looked towards Ione for sympathy, but Ione just looked a little blank. Ned Hump assumed it was because she had not fully understood, and he went on to explain again, differently and more simply.

'When I was very young,' he began, adding with the tact that Ione admired more every moment, 'much younger than you are now, there was a song. The words of this song went, as I recall—' and he began to sing in a soft, tuneless voice:

> '*You've got to have money in the bank, Frank.*
> *You've got to have money to start.*
> *When you have money in the bank, Frank,*
> *I'll give you my heart.*

And that, unfortunately for me, is how the lady feels.'

'I see,' said Ione.

And this time she did.

She took a deep breath.

'Would you like to come in for tea?' she invited him.

He, in his turn, took a deep breath. He narrowed his eyes.

'Must I meet *her*?' he asked, in a voice brimming over with suspicion. 'I don't think I could face it. I've had a basinful of her nastiness already today.'

Ione used tact. It came easily to her, she found. She wondered if it were the same sort of skill as telling lies, which she was also very good at.

'No,' she reassured him. 'You needn't meet her at all. We could have our tea alone in the kitchen. Miss Hope always stays with Daddy in the study.'

She saw that he was still hesitating, still unconvinced.

'There are chocolate biscuits left over from yesterday,' she tempted him. They always had chocolate biscuits on her last day of term.

He was lost.

Scrambling to his feet, he stretched out a hand to her.

'Come, my lady,' he said.

She took his hand and rose, with as much grace as she could muster, from the floor. She knew that he had badly wanted to say 'Come, Miss Muffet,' and had controlled himself at the very last moment. She thought that was very kind of him. She suffered from her name a lot.

24

'My Christian name is Ione,' she told him, as clearly and as unashamedly as he had told her his, before.

'I was hoping you would mention it,' he said. 'It seemed a little late in our flourishing relationship just brutally to ask.'

He kept her hand as they crossed the lawn, until they reached the sundial. Here, he dropped it in order to walk twice around the sundial, reading the inscription aloud as he circled it.

'Seize the present moment,' he read out, in a sing-song voice. 'The evening hour is nigh.'

He sighed, and strode off again in the direction of the back door. She thought he must know their garden pretty well.

'That's always been another of my problems,' she heard him mutter.

3

It was the daily help, Mrs Phipps's, day off, and the kitchen table was still cluttered with the lunch things that Ione hadn't yet cleared away.

Droopy bits of lettuce were draped over discarded tomato stalks, and little lumps of potato stuck to plates that had not yet been put on to the draining board, out of the way. There was a shallow pool of tinned peaches juice under the pepper mill, and an aspirin just on the edge, looking a little like a tiny white boat about to be launched on a trip to a monster light-house.

The floor, however, looked fairly clean. Mandy had had a quick lick-round before she went off to the study for her afternoon sleep.

Ned Hump did not seem to notice squalor. He just rooted around in the larder until he found the right biscuit tin. There were several in there, stacked up in a tottery pile in one corner; but most were empty. He found the right one, and pulled out a large packet of chocolate biscuits. Then he sat down at the table, out of Ione's way, and began to munch his way through. Ione was relieved that he did not seem to be the bread-and-butter-first sort. She always cut the loaf crooked, especially if, like today's, it was very fresh. Mrs Phipps refused to let them buy sliced loaves. She said they cost a whole penny more, and it was a cheat.

Ione began to set a tray for her father and Miss Hope. She tried, as she did it, to think of Miss Hope as Caroline; but it wasn't too easy, and she had never tried it before. She thought that Miss Hope would probably soon agree to be Mrs Hump anyway, so it wasn't worth making the effort of getting used to the change twice.

She filled the teapot, and placed beside it a mug, a cup and saucer, milk, sugar and a small plate of coconut biscuits. These were the only other sort of biscuits in the house, and she had decided to save all the chocolate ones for Ned Hump.

As she picked up the tray, Ned Hump jumped to his feet. He rushed to the door, and swung it open for her, towering above her as she passed by into the hall.

'Forgive me for not carrying it in for you,' he said, sounding truly concerned. 'But I just could not face the lady at this moment. I have been spurned and insulted enough for one day.'

Ione trailed along the hall, with its faded, fraying

carpet and its blotchy, damp-stained wallpaper. Since Professor Muffet could not see these frays and stains, he did nothing whatsoever about them; and Ione took them for granted. As long as she could remember, they had always been there.

She reached the far end, and pushed the study door open with her shoulder. It was a swing-open door, so that Mandy could get in and out, without a great fuss.

When they heard her come in, Miss Hope stopped typing, and Professor Muffet stopped telling her what to type.

'At *last*,' said Professor Muffet. 'We were gasping.'

'How lovely,' said Miss Hope. 'Shall I pour?'

Ione set the tray in front of her, and stepped back to the doorway. She watched as Miss Hope coped, as efficiently as she coped with everything, with the pouring. Miss Hope was a little *too* efficient at times, Ione thought; but for all she tried, standing there in the doorway, she couldn't imagine Miss Hope being nasty to anybody, and especially not to someone as gentle and thoughtful as Ned Hump.

She wondered if perhaps there had been some mistake. Perhaps Miss Hope wasn't Caroline at all, but had a twin sister with that name. Ione tried one more time to think of her as Caroline. It didn't work.

Miss Hope passed Professor Muffet a large, stripey blue mug full of tea. Ione's father always drank out of a mug at home. He hated having to use a cup and saucer. After he had lifted the cup to sip from it, he always used to forget on which arm of the chair, or on which part of the desk or floor, he had left the saucer; and then he had to waste time, feeling around for it. Sometimes he gave up, and forgot about the saucer entirely, and then trod upon it later. So now he always preferred to use a mug.

Professor Muffet was forty-one years old and untidy. He became more and more scruffy-looking as the day went by, not being able to see himself in mirrors as he passed, and straighten himself up a little. He did not have a beard, though it would have been easier – he used an electric razor instead. He usually shaved badly, but more from not trying than from being incapable. One can, after all, *feel* stubble.

He had been blind since he was six years old. He could remember all about colours, and what the sea looked like, and so he was easy enough to talk to about that sort of thing. He liked going for long walks, either with Mandy or with Ione if Mandy was too tired, or with both. And most evenings he played the piano, sometimes late into the night. That was when he most missed his wife, Doris, who used to comment on his wrong notes, and sometimes he even wished he had another wife.

Ione's mother had died when Ione was three years old, so there had always been housekeepers and nannies as long as she could remember. The old ones were always called housekeepers, and known as Mrs Something, and always left because some relation or another had fallen ill, and needed nursing; and the young ones were called nannies, and known by their Christian names, and always left to get married.

When the last one, a nanny, had left a few months before, Ione had said, '*Must* we have somebody else? Can't we just be us?'

Her father had said, 'She was nice to you, wasn't she? She didn't upset you, I hope.'

'Oh, no,' said Ione. 'It's just that I thought, now I'm so much older, perhaps we could manage, just the two of us.'

Professor Muffet had twiddled his fingers and patted the dog and fingered his tea mug and straightened his files, and wondered if anything anyone *wanted* could possibly be *good* for them, if they were only Ione's age; and at last he had said, 'I'll tell you what. I'll tell you what we'll do. We'll *assume* that we're going to get another nanny. But we'll just not *look* very hard for one. And in the meantime, we'll ask Mrs Phipps to come in from the village more often and do some of the cooking as well as the cleaning. And we'll get more of the groceries delivered. And in term-time, you must stay at school for lunch. How about that? Will that do?'

'I think that's just right,' Ione had said.

And after that, Ione had even begun to learn to cook, as well as to learn braille. She felt very strongly that she should try and be some help to her father. Sometimes, in the past, she had been dreadful.

There had been the time, for example, when Ione was five, and had first realised that if she kept dead still, and hardly breathed, then Daddy couldn't see or find her, although she could see him. She had often frightened him very badly this way, when the nanny was on her day off, or in another room.

She still remembered one particular day, one winter's afternoon, when she had pushed over a tea-trolley from running too fast.

There had been the most enormous, resounding crash. Splinters of shattered glass, and pieces of broken tea-cups had sprayed far and wide over the carpet. Sugar had dredged the sofa cushions. Tea-leaves had bespattered the curtains. It had all been a dreadful mess, and she knew she was to blame, for not looking where she was running.

She had shrunk back into the curtains, held her breath and frozen.

'Ione!' her father had shouted. 'Ione – are you all right?'

But she was terrified because she had broken so many things, and spilt so much tea on to everything, and she kept quite, quite still, rigid with fear.

Panicking, her father had dropped on to his knees, amid the broken crockery and the damp patches on the carpet; and he had felt frantically around on the floor, trying to find her, calling her name all the time. He thought she must have hurt herself badly, and perhaps be lying somewhere out of reach, unconscious.

And she became more and more frightened by his strange behaviour. She was, after all, only five. She had shrunk back, further and further, into the curtains, as silent as a ghost.

Suddenly, he had seemed to despair of ever finding her.

'Ione,' he had whispered. 'Please, love . . .'

She had let out her breath, then; and he had heard, and reached out for her. He had pulled her into his arms, and stood up, and carried her, trembling all over, into the big red leather chair. And while she had cried and cried, he had stroked her hair and whispered to her that it didn't matter at all, not one bit, until the nanny at last came in from the garden, where she had been rescuing some washing from the rain, and had cleared up all the mess in no time at all.

Ione had never been as bad as that again. But even after all these years, she had been surprised when Daddy agreed not to look terribly hard for a new nanny for her. Ione knew full well that if you didn't look terribly hard, you never found one at all.

Now Miss Hope, teapot in hand and floppy ear-rings swaying, was smiling in her usual friendly fashion towards Ione, who was still lurking in the doorway.

'Where's your cup?' Miss Hope asked. 'Aren't you joining us today?'

'I don't think so, thank you,' said Ione. 'I think I had better go and give Mandy some fresh water. I think she's been without for most of the day.'

For all her doubts about the morals of lying, Ione was most accomplished at the art.

By the time she returned to the kitchen, Ned Hump had ploughed his way through all but three of the chocolate biscuits. These three, after some thought and a considerable act of will, he had placed on a nearby plate, and left for his hostess.

He was sitting, sunk in gloom, with his head bent, shredding the cellophane of the biscuit packet, and letting the pieces drop on to the floor, where they rustled softly in the draught from the door.

Ione went round the table and stood on the other side, facing him.

'Coffee's easier . . .' she said hopefully. (There was only one teapot.)

'I'd *much* prefer coffee,' he said helpfully, though his voice sounded downcast.

Ione put more water into the kettle, and put it on again.

'It must be hateful to be in love,' she said, spooning coffee granules into mugs.

'Hateful,' he agreed. 'Especially when one has the misfortune to love an old bat like her ladyship.'

Ione stared.

'Do you wish you'd never met her?' she asked, at last.

'No,' he said. 'But that's love for you.'

'She must drive you mad.'

'She does.'

Ione poured boiling water into the mugs. 'She does Daddy, too,' she said, soothingly.

Ned Hump lifted his head. He did not look soothed. He looked confused and anxious.

'I beg your pardon?' he said.

'She drives Daddy mad, too,' Ione repeated.

'Ah, yes,' said Ned Hump, and relapsed into being downcast. He buried his nose into his coffee mug. Then he lifted it out again.

'Why?' he asked.

'Why what?'

'Why does she drive Professor Muffet mad?'

Ione tried to think of her father as Professor Muffet. She found it even more difficult than thinking of Miss Hope as Caroline. She wondered *why* she always thought of Miss Hope as Miss Hope. Miss Hope couldn't, after all, be older than Ned Hump, and she could think of Ned Hump as Ned with no trouble at all. She tried, just as an experiment, to think of Ned as Mr Hump, and she lost herself in a tangle of assorted thoughts.

Patiently, Ned Hump asked his question all over again.

'*Why* does Caroline drive your father mad?'

Ione considered.

'He says she's not dependable,' she said.

'He's dead right, she's not.'

'Daddy says she's always ringing him up at the last minute, saying she can't come at all; or, if she can, it won't be for hours and hours.'

'He gets that too, does he?' asked Ned, with interest. He seemed to be cheering visibly. 'Why does *he* put up with it?' He sighed. 'It's not as if *he* were in love with her, too.'

Ione thought. He *might* be. After all, Miss Hope was awfully pretty, though her father only had *her* word for that. And she had a lovely low, chokey voice. But then, Daddy was far too old for Miss Hope. She decided that the obvious answer must be the right one, after all.

'He *has* to,' she said. 'She's the only person the Agency could find, when Miss Nettleton left, who could transcribe from braille, *and* come and live near here so she could come and do it every day.' She drank some of her coffee. 'And Daddy says that she's very good indeed at the job, and doesn't shuffle all his papers up, out of spite, like the last one did. But she's only good when she's here. And she's so often *not* here. And so Daddy gets into rages – goes quite mad, like when he gets letters telling him to hurry up and do things – and he says terrible things about women, and Miss Hope particularly. And then sometimes, when he's really in a rage, he starts on about that loon of a sardine of hers.'

'That *what*?'

Ned Hump was totally baffled.

'That loon of a sardine who lures her away from her work.' Ione reached over the table and picked up one of the few remaining chocolate biscuits.

Ned Hump ran a long finger round and round the rim of his coffee mug, clockwise, dissolving the sugar that had stuck to its edge. He was still baffled.

'I knew she kept a cat,' he said. 'I didn't know she kept a sardine. Especially not an ailing one that she has to stay home and nurse. Indeed, I didn't think that *anybody* kept sardines – except in tins, of course, for unexpected guests.'

He began to run a different finger round the rim of his mug, in the other direction. 'You would think,' he said thoughtfully, 'that she would find herself hard pressed to keep her cat from devouring the sardine. I imagine cats are most partial to sardines.'

He stopped rubbing his mug altogether, and looked up. 'But Miss Caroline Hope was ever resourceful,' he concluded. 'If anybody in the world could keep both a cat and a sardine in the same flat, without a catfight, it would be her ladyship.'

He sunk his chin into his hands.

'Blast her to bits,' he added, as an afterthought.

Ione had finished eating her biscuit now, and could speak again.

'She doesn't keep sardines at all,' she said. 'Nobody does. They're always dead to begin with.'

'They're not *born* in tins, you know,' said Ned Hump.

'You know what I mean,' said Ione.

Ned Hump lowered his head, as a kind of apology.

Ione went on with her explanation.

'That loon of a sardine is just Daddy's nickname for one of his students at the university,' she said. 'He says Miss Hope is always letting him down so that she can rush off, at no notice at all, to parties and films and things with this student. It's the *student* he calls that loon of a sardine.'

Ione was deep into her second biscuit now, so she neither saw the stormclouds of comprehension gathering on Ned Hump's brow, nor noticed the sudden glitter in his large brown eyes. She sailed on, after swallowing, into a deeper and deeper lack of tact.

'Daddy calls this student a loon of a sardine because he has . . .' – she took a huge breath, and tried to remember the exact phrase her father always used – '. . . because he has the most extraordinarily loony views Daddy can imagine *anyone* holding, on the Early Sardinian Trade Routes. Daddy says he sometimes even fears for this student's sanity.'

Ione stretched out her hand for the last biscuit. That was when she saw his face. That was when, at long last, the exact phrase rang the exact bell. Early Sardinian Trade Routes. The exact same phrase that Ned Hump had used. It was exactly what he said he disagreed with her father about, when they met in the summer-house.

Ione's hand froze over the last biscuit. Her face went scarlet.

She sat there, unable to move, appalled by her slowness and her lack of tact.

'You . . .?' she faltered, at last. '*You're* the *loon?*'

She could hardly believe it. But of course it all fitted in.

Ned Hump rose to his feet.

First, she thought he was going to hit her. Then she thought he was going to stalk out in a huff.

But he just stuck out his hand.

'Meet,' he said, formally. 'Meet your first walking, talking sardine.' He shook her hand. '*Loon* of a sardine, that is,' he corrected himself.

Then he bowed, like something out of a tin, and she nearly fell off her chair, laughing almost as loudly as he was.

4

They were laughing so loudly that neither of them heard the door's faint click, and the quiet swoosh of draught as it swung open.

Neither of them noticed Professor Muffet, standing framed in the doorway, the small plate of coconut biscuits in his hand.

Their bout of laughter did, however, finally die away. And it was only then that Professor Muffet spoke.

'Do I hear *two* laughs?' he enquired of the air around him. 'To be more explicit, do I hear, merged in companionable merriment, the laughter of my daughter and the laughter of Ned Hump?'

'Oh, Lord,' said Ned Hump. All of a sudden, he looked as though he hadn't laughed in weeks.

Professor Muffet raised an eyebrow. The left one. He only ever raised the left one when he only raised one. It was the only one he could raise by itself.

'What are you about, young man?' he asked. 'Settled in my kitchen, carousing with my daughter, the evening before your examination?'

'Oh, Lord,' said Ned Hump again. He was totally taken aback. He could not think how Professor Muffet could have known it was him, solely from hearing his laugh. He was not aware of how skilled Professor Muffet had become at guessing whose voice he was hearing, even in an unexpected place and even from a shout or a laugh. Ned might have expected to have his voice recognised in the university, asking a question after a lecture, or offering to take Mandy out for a quick run. But to have his laugh pinned down in a kitchen where he had never been before, and where he had no business to be, put him out rather.

So Ned stared fixedly at the last chocolate biscuit, and wondered what he could say. Finally, he said, 'We met in the summer-house. And now I am eating your chocolate biscuits. Your daughter is very kindly feeding me up. Before the ordeal.'

He turned to Ione and added, politely, in explanation, 'By the ordeal, I mean my examination. It is tomorrow, at half past three. I don't have to *write* anything – that part was all over last month. But I have to sit in front of a tableful of historians, including your father, and answer their questions on what I did write, last month, without appearing to them to be an idiot. And on this exam tomorrow my whole future depends. For only afterwards will I know if I have a good enough examination result to get a good enough job to get Roofs Over Heads and Good Starts In Life and Little Somethings To Put Away In Case Of Rainy Days, and therefore the hand in marriage of Miss Caroline Hope herself.'

He listed off Miss Hope's Notions in exactly the same order as he had done before, in the summer-house. Ione thought he must think and worry about them a lot to have them off so pat.

Ione gazed at him, her eyes brimming with pity behind her fringe. She thought it was all one of the saddest things that she had ever heard.

But Professor Muffet leaned against the draining board, trying hard not to let his intense amusement show. The plate of coconut biscuits in his hand slipped into a rather dangerous angle.

Ned Hump regarded the last chocolate biscuit even more moodily than before. Clearly, listing the Notions had depressed him utterly. Then, without thinking, for it was by rights Ione's, he reached out his hand and took the biscuit from the plate. He made deliberate, rounded fingerprints on the chocolate-coated side, and then inspected them.

'Of course,' he went on, bitterly, 'the likelihood of my doing well tomorrow is not too great. For I am told that I hold views on the Early Sardinian Trade Routes that should not be held by a sane man, that are unacceptable even to the sparsely in-formed, and that befit only a crank.' He added, for the benefit of Ione who had not understood a word,

'In short, your father already thinks I am an idiot.'

'I'm sure he doesn't,' said Ione, with prompt tact.

'I *do*,' said Professor Muffet. 'I am convinced of it.'

Professor Muffet was usually most polite, but he had been arguing with Ned Hump about the Early Sardinian Trade Routes for a whole term now, and it was getting to be a very sore point with him. In his agitation, he allowed the plate in his hand to slide even further at an angle, and the coconut biscuits fell, one by one, off it.

He did not notice that the plate had become suddenly a little lighter. His eyes glittered. He was getting on his hobby-horse.

'Hump here holds that Gesualdo of Punta Lamormara who, I would remind you, Ione, would only have been *seven years old* at the time in question—' Ione looked blankly at her father;

'*Only* if you take Punkle's calculation of the year of Gesualdo's birth to be the correct one,' put in Ned Hump.

'Which you don't?'

'Which I don't.'

'Then you are an idiot,' said Ione's father, triumphantly, as though his point had been proved beyond all doubt. 'You're totally insane. And what are you doing in my kitchen, maniac?'

But Ned Hump did not reply to this taunt. He had suddenly dived headlong under the table, and was cowering behind Ione's knees, clutching at her jeans, trying desperately to hide all six feet three inches of himself.

For Miss Caroline Hope had just appeared in the doorway.

She had come to see what was happening, and why the Professor had been away for so long just looking for chocolate biscuits.

As she came in, she took the empty plate that had once held the coconut ones, from his hand, and put it down safely on the draining board, out of the way.

'Did you eat *all* of them?' she asked him, with interest. 'Every last one? I thought you didn't care for them, either. I thought that was why you came back here. To change them.'

She turned to Ione. 'Aren't there any of the chocolate ones left over from yesterday?' she asked her. Then she caught sight of the remains of the empty packet, crumpled on the top of the biscuit-tin lid, and the crumby plate.

'Goodness, you glutton,' said Miss Hope to Ione. 'You've pigged every last one. There must have been at least a dozen, too.'

A choking noise sounded underneath the table. Ione coughed, to try and disguise it, but Miss Hope was not an idiot.

She bent down low and peered under the table.

'Why, Ned,' she said, sweet as sugared poison. 'How kind of you to crawl in.'

'Oh, Lord,' Ned Hump's voice wafted up from somewhere underneath Ione. Then he despaired, and clambered out.

'Oh, Lord.' Professor Muffet's voice wafted over

from somewhere near the sink where, weak from laughing, he was clutching at the draining board for support. And *he* was only *imagining* the scene.

Blotches of the last chocolate digestive had made their way all over Ned Hump's unusual tie. They made the pattern even more bizarre.

Miss Hope glared venomously at Ned Hump. 'What are you doing in this house, you meddlesome, nosey moron?' she demanded.

Ione stared, astonished, at Miss Hope. She was quite a different person. All vague thoughts of possible twin-sisters vanished from Ione's brain. This was the Miss Hope she knew, and yet this was nastiness indeed – sheer, neat nastiness.

Ione saw for the first time what Ned meant when he said to her that he had had a basinful of the lady already that day.

Ione turned her eyes curiously on to Ned. He was looking defeated and gormless, pulling threads from the ends of his tie, and then wrapping them tightly round his fingertips. From time to time, his large, spaniel's eyes looked up and shone mournfully at his beloved.

Ione acted. She remembered that, come what may, Ned loved Caroline. So she acted.

'Mandy chased him in here,' she said, decisively. 'She must have got out of the garden somehow. And he was just walking down the road, and Mandy went mad, he says, quite berserk, and chased him in through the gate and over the lawn. He was scared she might bite him sc he banged on the kitchen door, and I let him in, and we barricaded the door against Mandy, but threw her some chocolate digestives to calm her down.'

She stopped. She saw the blatant disbelief in Miss Hope's ice-hard eyes. Ione finished, a little lamely, 'We think that it was because he had been near a terrier – perhaps near Mrs Phipps's terrier further up the hill, and he somehow got the smell of terrier on to his jeans. Mandy *hates* terriers.'

Ione's voice died away again. It never did to add too much icing to a lie.

But she needn't have bothered herself in the first place. Miss Hope had clearly not believed a single word of the tale.

'That dog,' said Miss Hope, icily, 'is so fat that she could no more chase Ned Hump than fly.'

Ione was momentarily defeated. But since Ned Hump still appeared to be incapable of defending himself against the blows, she set off on another rescue tactic. This time, she decided to try distraction.

'Mandy *is* fat,' she admitted, gabbling cheerfully, as though she thought that by the sheer speed of her voice alone she could carry all their minds far away from the issue under discussion. 'Daddy tried to put her on to a diet once, just before you came, Miss Hope. He only let her eat one meal a day, and no scraps at all. So we had to keep the kitchen floor well-swept all the time. It was all such a bother, Mrs Phipps swore that she'd leave. But Mandy didn't get any thinner at all. She just got fearfully hungry and bad-tempered, and refused to lead Daddy all the way to the bus-stop any more.'

She turned to her father for support; but he could give her none. He was almost doubled up with laughter. So Ione carried on alone.

'*Yes*, you do. You remember. She began stopping half-way up Hanger's Hill and you couldn't budge her, not one inch, because she was such a tub; and the bus driver only stopped because he *knew* you, and then after a week or so, the conductor said you'd *have* to get Mandy off the diet, or whatever it was that was making her act so oddly, because the Company had told him that they mustn't stop the bus for you on that hill any more, because it was a bend and *far* too dangerous, and the lives of all the other passengers were at risk. So *you* said that since there were only two other regular passengers on that bus anyhow, and one of those was only . . .'

Ned Hump had laid a hand gently on Ione's shoulder.

'It's no use,' he told her. 'I've tried it often enough myself. It doesn't work. Nothing does. Nothing works with her when she's in a mood.'

Miss Hope's eyes flashed green fire.

'Ooooh!' she choked. 'You tiny-minded, pea-brained *pin-head*! You think you're so *noble*, don't you? That's what gets me. And yet you won't do *one tiny thing* for me. You say you love me, and yet you won't do *one tiny thing*.'

'*One tiny thing?*' Ned shouted back. '*One tiny thing!*'
His voice reached a shriek. '"My whole fortune's
fee", more like.' He paused, to let his voice come
down an octave, and then swung round to face his
tutor.

Professor Muffet heard him move, and tried to put
his face straight.

'She wants me,' Ned told Professor Muffet, livid
with outrage, 'she wants me to *perjure* myself, to *ap-
pease*, to *conform*. She wants me, tomorrow, to *sell my
soul*. She wants me to tell giant great lies about what
I believe about the Early Sardinian Trade Routes,
just so, *if* we ever do get married – and I'm fast going
off the idea – then I'll have a good degree, so I'll get
a good job, so we'll have some good money, so we'll
be able to buy a good house, so we can fill it with
good fridges, and all that other rubbish.'

Caroline shrieked at him then, outraged in her
turn.

'It isn't the fridges,' she cried, almost in tears of
fury. 'I never even *mentioned* a fridge. It's your stupid
babies I'm worried about, Ned Hump. I've told you
before, and I'll tell you again and again and again,
I am *not* having your babies, and living under a
hedge.'

There fell, between the two of them, the silence of
exhaustion. And not for the first time either.

Professor Muffet pulled himself together and
stepped into the large, social hole that had been dug
in his kitchen.

'Ione,' he said, 'can you remember what I did with the whisky bottle?'

'Yes, I can,' said Ione. 'You hid it from Aunt Alice. You hid it in one of your Wellington boots.'

He asked her which one, but she did not answer. She was miles away, thinking. She was thinking that Miss Hope had quite a point, when you thought about it. Ione wouldn't care to bring up a family of babies under a hedge, either. They would be almost *bound* to catch pneumonia and die.

'So,' said Ione's father, with a large and obvious sigh, 'Hump and I will go to my study. Kindly keep us undisturbed until we emerge. If we do nothing else before night falls, we shall settle this question of the Early Sardinian Trade Routes, for once and for all. Follow me, Hump.'

Ned followed him, though reluctantly. They had been arguing about the Early Sardinian Trade Routes all term, and he was fed up with it all, too.

But as he passed Ione, he brightened up enough to blow her a kiss. And as he passed Miss Hope, he said, out of the corner of his mouth, 'Marry me, you stubborn old bat, and be my only sweet love foreverandevermore.'

'Push off, Ned,' said Miss Hope.

Ned stuck out his large tongue at her, and shambled off after Professor Muffet.

Ione watched him go. She wondered if even she might, just now and then, find him a little bit trying.

5

Left alone together, Ione and Miss Hope surveyed the wreckage on the kitchen table and on the floor. Then they sat down.

'I think,' said Ione, surprising herself with her own frankness, 'I think that *I* would marry him even if I did have to live under a hedge. He's more lovely than not.'

Miss Hope yawned. Her temper had quite passed over, leaving her as sunny as usual.

'Do you have any other drink in the house?' she asked. 'Anything that isn't closeted in with those two, I mean. Cooking sherry, or something? I really don't see why they should be the only ones to have a drink, I really don't.'

'I know we have cooking sherry,' said Ione, 'because we use it for trifles when Aunt Alice comes. Aunt Alice loves trifles, and Mrs Phipps always puts loads of sherry in them, so that Aunt Alice will go off to sleep after lunch and leave her in peace.' She went into the larder and began looking for it. 'But it's probably ancient by now,' she added. 'Aunt Alice hasn't been for ages.'

'It keeps,' said Caroline. 'Sometimes it even improves.'

'I've never drunk before,' said Ione. 'Except at Christmas and New Year, and things like that.'

'Oh, well,' said Miss Hope philosophically, 'better to start off on a life of vice with me than with—' she paused, and then finished '—than with anyone less dependable.'

'Daddy doesn't think you're at all dependable,' said Ione, her tact slipping. 'And neither does Ned.'

She searched around the pantry shelves and felt behind the breakfast cereals, until she found, behind the gravy-browning bottle and the soy sauce, the cooking-sherry bottle. It was covered with dust, and quite full, though the label was peeling off on one side.

They drank the sherry from mugs. It seemed simpler, if not as elegant, as drinking out of glasses. And besides, all the sherry glasses were in the study, from which loud, aggressive noises had begun to issue. It sounded as though the question of the Early Sardinian Trade Routes was being very thoroughly thrashed out.

Ione looked at her watch. It was a quarter past eight.

Ione looked at her watch. It was whizzing round and round and round. The face was spinning in one direction, and the numbers were spinning in the other. They were not spinning fast, but fast enough not to pin down long enough to read. And the big and little hands seemed temporarily to have disappeared.

'What time is it?' she asked.

Miss Hope, who had, during Ione's second mugful of cooking sherry, inexplicably and without any warning at all, turned into being Caroline, narrowed her dark green eyes. Being more practised in drunkenness than Ione was, she did not even attempt to tell the time from her tiny gold wristwatch, but peered through drooping eyelids at the large round electric wall clock, with the huge, orange numbers.

'It is a quarter past twelve,' she said.

'Lord,' said Ione. She was astonished.

They had been playing poker, which Caroline had taught her, for four whole hours, using a pack of cards which Caroline had found at the back of the spoon drawer. Since there were no matches to be found, they were playing with spoons; and the table was now covered with spoons – apostle spoons, tea spoons, serving spoons, wooden spoons, two ladles, and even an ice-cream dispenser that Ione had found on the larder floor. Caroline was winning. She had won every game so far.

Caroline now said, 'Are they still at it?'

They sat still, so that the table ceased rocking, and the spoons jangling. And from the study still came the sounds that Professor Muffet and Ned

Hump had been making all evening. And as they had drunk further and further down the whisky bottle, the sounds had become louder and louder.

As Caroline and Ione had drunk further and further down the cooking-sherry bottle, they had noticed the noise less and less.

'*Why* won't you marry him?' Ione asked Caroline for at least the tenth time. She found it difficult, with her head swimming as it was, to remember exactly which questions she *had* asked Caroline, and which she had only *thought* of asking her.

Strangely, she did not seem to remember any of Caroline's answers at all.

'Why don't I marry him?' Caroline's voice was thick and slurry-furry, on top of its usual chokiness. 'I've *told* you. I've told you *over* and *over* again. I *will* marry him. Put that ladle back at *once*. It's from *my* pile. I'll marry him *when* he has a job.'

Caroline reached down and picked a piece of coconut biscuit from where it was wedged, in the handle of the cupboard under the draining board.

'Blast him to bits,' she added, in just the same tone of voice that *he* had used when he wished the same on her.

Ione smiled to herself. She thought that Caroline and Ned would go wonderfully together, married.

Caroline licked the biscuit, experimentally. 'Tastes so arid, coconut does,' she said. 'Like a desert.' She licked it again. 'If you don't like deserts, that is,' she said. 'I mean, if you don't like coconut.'

Suddenly she froze, dramatically, one finger raised high in the air.

'Sshhh,' she said. 'Listen.'

Ione listened. She could hear her head going round, but that was inside her. Outside her, there was nothing to be heard. Not one sound. Even the spoons had shut up for the moment.

'Lord,' muttered Ione. 'They've killed one another stone dead.'

'*Stoned* dead, more like,' said the more experienced Caroline, and she giggled.

She placed the licked and soggy piece of biscuit carefully back upon the draining-board cupboard handle, where she had found it, and rose, a little unsteadily, to her feet. With biscuity fingers, she pushed the hair from her eyes, tangling coconut crumbs up in her curls.

'We should go and investigate,' she told Ione. 'We should go and see exactly what has happened.'

Caroline led the way down the hall, and Ione stumbled behind her. It was, Ione found, much more difficult to walk than just to sit at a kitchen table. The walls seemed to surge in on her, and then rush away again. Her feet seemed to keep wanting to take off to one side, on their own.

Ione was concentrating so hard on her own crab-like progress, that she did not notice when Caroline came to a halt, and so she fell heavily against her.

Caroline, being more experienced, held firm.

'The keyhole,' suggested Ione, in a conspiratorial whisper.

'There is none,' Caroline pointed out. 'It is a swing door.'

She spoke slowly and clearly, as though she had to work hard to choose the right words, and then say them in exactly the right order and at an equal level of loudness.

Caroline pushed the swing door open a fraction, and peered through the crack she had made. She could only see one small corner of the room, and neither Ned nor Professor Muffet was, at that moment, in that small corner.

Caroline gave a large, dramatic sigh.

She tried to push the door open a fraction more. Still it would not give. She pushed harder. It remained firm.

On the other side of the door, Mandy was awakening from a deep sleep because of a strange and forceful pressure of cold door upon her rump. She tried to ignore it, and carry on with her dream, but the pressure increased, colder and more forceful. Mandy came to her senses enough to rise, shake herself and pad off to her other favourite late-night sleeping patch, under the Professor's desk.

At that very moment, Caroline pushed one last time, even harder.

Since the obstruction had taken itself off, the door swung wide open, fast, and Caroline careered into the room, closely followed by Ione, who had been leaning upon her for support.

The two surveyed the room. It seemed to be swaying slightly, but it was definitely empty. The French windows, however, were ajar and the curtains were billowing gently in the night's breeze.

'They must have stepped out for a walk,' said the more experienced Caroline. She picked up the whisky bottle from where it stood, upon a pile of papers. It left a faint golden ring on the top one.

'Empty,' she said. 'And so the walk may well prove all but fatal. Fresh air can be the worst thing imaginable, after a lot of hard drink.'

'Doesn't it clear your head?' said Ione, who rather wanted to go out and try to find them. 'I thought that it did.'

'In the end it does,' Caroline admitted. 'But often, only after it has made you feel a lot worse first.'

The last two words – the sound of them – seemed to appeal to her greatly. 'Worse forse, worse forse, worse forse,' she sang gently to herself, swaying round in tight little circles, cradling the empty whisky bottle. Her drunkenness seemed to come over her in waves, unlike Ione's, which stayed at a steady level of not quite being in control, and feeling things deeply.

'But it's so *nice* out,' said Ione, feeling this deeply. 'There's moonshine, and stars all over.' She peered, wistfully, out of the gap in the French windows.

Caroline giggled again. 'Very well,' she said. 'Very

well. *We* shall go out, too. But I warn you, it may be dangerous. Just try not to take any breaths.'

They stepped out, and down the few verandah steps on to the lawn. Caroline was still clutching the whisky bottle. Ione was beginning to wonder if Caroline was more experienced, after all, or whether she had just poured into her mug more of the cooking sherry than she had poured into Ione's.

'Where shall we go? Where shall we go?' demanded Caroline. '*You* should know. It's your garden.'

Ione considered.

'We *could* go to the summer-house,' she said. She wanted to find her father and Ned Hump, and she thought that they might possibly be there. They did not appear to be anywhere in the shrubbery, from the lack of rustlings there; and they were clearly nowhere in the open. That only left the summer-house. But Ione added, dubiously, 'It might be a little scarey there, at this time of night.' Her mind somersaulted backwards, to earlier that day. 'There might be a stranger, lurking there,' she said. 'Like Ned did.'

Caroline giggled. 'A loon,' she said. 'Another loon, under the moon, whom we may meet soon, though it's well past June.'

She seemed to be in a very rhymy mood, Ione thought.

'*I* shall protect you,' Caroline said.

So they plodded carefully over the dew-sodden grass, towards the tangly end of the garden, and the summer-house. Ione's head was swirling. She felt just a little sick.

But just as they were only a few yards away, the moon shot out from behind a cloud, and lit the whole scene up, in a glimmering, pale-silver way, and Ione's sickness was completely forgotten.

Both of them gazed, in admiration and wonder. Caroline had never seen the summer-house before, and Ione had never seen it looking at all like this.

It shimmered. It gleamed. It looked a thousand years old.

'My!' breathed Caroline. 'It has hundreds and hundreds of sides.'

Ione's head was settling now. Caroline had been quite right, as usual. After you felt worse, you felt better.

'It hasn't hundreds of sides,' she said. 'Don't be silly. It *couldn't* have that many sides. It has eight. There look more, in this queer light, but in fact there are only eight.'

Caroline said, 'There are at least a dozen.'

Ione said, 'There are exactly eight.'

Caroline insisted, 'There are a dozen.'

Ione said loftily, 'It is octagonal. So there are eight. You can walk round it and count them, if you don't want to believe me.'

Suddenly, it was very important to Ione that Caroline *should* believe her. This was partly because her mind was placing an exaggerated importance on trivial things, because of the sherry; and partly because she was more than a little fed up with being the youngest person in the house, and knowing the least. And this she *did* know. The summer-house had eight sides. It was *her* place. She spent *hours* there. She should know.

'Very well,' said Caroline. 'I shall walk round and count.'

This was easier said than done, since this was the tangly end of the garden; but Caroline forced her way bravely through the thorny brambles, and the prickly briers, and the stumpy little two-year-old chestnut trees that the gardener hadn't yet noticed, and uprooted.

And on each side of the summer-house, as she passed by, Caroline delivered a loud thump, counting aloud.

At last, after what seemed to Ione to be a noisy age, she appeared again, round to the right, and leaned against the side that Ione was marking by leaning against it herself.

Caroline was completely dishevelled. 'You are right,' she panted. 'There are eight. And my tights are in shreds.'

Ione giggled. Then the moon swam out again even shinier than before, and lit them up, and everything around them, almost to brightness.

Ione gasped.

There on the summer-house door, scored heavily into the warped and paint-flaked wood, was some lettering that she had never seen before.

'Look,' she whispered, and pointed.

Caroline looked first at Ione's finger, and then she pulled herself together, and looked where Ione was pointing. Then she gasped, too.

'My!' she whispered back, horrified. 'Look what he's *done*. It'll be there for *ever*.'

He had hacked, in huge, uneven letters, deep into the door's panels, his drunken, heartfelt message:

Ned Hump loves Caroline. This is more than true. XXXXX

Caroline stood dead still. Her cheeks went pink. Then she stretched out her fingers and ran them gently over each letter in turn, whispering the message softly to herself again, as she did so. 'Ned Hump loves Caroline. This is more than true. Kiss, kiss, kiss, kiss, kiss.'

Then she sat down on the step, which was cold and damp from the dew, and she burst into noisy, sentimental tears.

Ione sat down beside her. She wasn't sure why Caroline was crying, so she said, because it was the only thing she could think of to say, and she really meant it, 'How super for you.'

Caroline's sobs subsided, gradually. Ione had said just the right thing. While Caroline calmed down, Ione gazed around the moonlit tangles. *She* wouldn't have cried, she thought, if it had been written for *her*. Well, maybe she would . . .

Caroline said, 'How super for me. How super for me.'

She sat on the cold, damp step, and cried and giggled.

Once again, the thought crossed Ione's mind that Caroline might not, perhaps, be nearly as experienced as she made herself out to be.

They might, Ione thought, have sat there all night, had not a strange noise suddenly floated across the lawn, towards them.

Ione shook Caroline into quiet.

'Listen,' she said.

From out of the shadowy night came the sound of singing – tuneless, happy, mindless singing:

> *'Here we go round the sundial bush,*
> *The sundial bush, the sundial bush;*
> *Here we go round the sundial bush,*
> *On a warm and moony evening.'*

Ione dragged Caroline to her feet and through the narrow path between the brambles down on to the edge of the lawn. The moon was still out, and strong, and in the eerie half-light that it cast, they saw a weird sight.

Ione's father and Ned Hump had come from nowhere, out into the middle of the lawn. Like two untidy scarecrows, suddenly brought to life, they were careering round and round the sundial, holding hands across it to keep one another upright and revolving. And as they wheeled and spun, they howled out to the moon their warped nursery rhyme, over and over again.

Caroline pulled herself together.

'Couple of loons,' she said, acidly.

She appeared to be quite put out. Perhaps, Ione thought, after the loving message they had just found, she had imagined Ned to be alone and palely loitering, like the knight-at-arms in the poem.

Caroline turned and took Ione's hand.

'You and I shall return to the house,' she said, in a distinctly school-mistressy tone of voice that Ione strongly resented. 'We shall find beds and we shall go to sleep.'

She led the way indoors again, stepping silently round the edge of the lawn, shrouded by the lilacs, in order, Ione assumed, that they should not be noticed; but she took the trouble to walk with her nose stuck high in the air, just in case they were.

Ione went with her most unwillingly, dragging her feet. She could hardly take her eyes off the sight of her father and Ned Hump, dancing their crazy dance. She rustled against all the bushes that she could, in the hope that they would hear, and call them over. But both Ned and her father were making so much noise that they could hardly hear each other, let alone anyone else.

Ione stumbled on the steps into the house, from looking too far backwards over her shoulder, whilst being firmly pulled by Caroline.

Safe in the study again, Caroline stopped and took her nose out of the air for a second.

'One blind, and one blind drunk,' she said coldly.

Then she softened a little. 'Is there any chance that your father will hurt himself, Ione? To hell with Ned.'

Ione tried to think. She found it difficult, with Caroline in all these moods, one after another, and standing so close. Ione found Caroline's sudden changes of mood quite exhausting. No wonder, she thought to herself, no *wonder* Ned Hump is so *thin*.

Finally she suggested, 'We could send Mandy out. Mandy'll keep an eye on him.'

Caroline dug a reluctant Mandy out from under the desk, with her foot. 'Wake up, dog,' she said. 'Get out there. Earn your keep.'

Although tipped out on to the carpet like a large grey beachball, Mandy ignored Caroline in the most dignified way she could think of. She pretended that she was still fast asleep.

So Ione tried. She bent down and tickled Mandy's ears. 'Go find Daddy,' she whispered. 'Go to Daddy. Fetch Daddy.'

With a yawn, Mandy pulled herself upright. She licked Ione's nose wetly, mostly in order to snub Caroline, and plodded obediently out of the French windows and over the lawn. She sat down again, still yawning, a few yards from the sundial, just out of danger from any passing, flailing limbs, and waited patiently for the lunatic dance to finish.

'What a clever dog she is,' said Ione proudly, watching from the window. The lick had surprised and delighted her.

'Ought to be,' said Caroline. 'Guide-dogs cost enough. And they take *ages* to train.' She pushed open the door into the hall. 'Where shall *I* sleep?' she asked. 'I can't possibly go home. All the buses stopped *hours* ago.'

Caroline was right. She couldn't possibly go home. Her drunkenness kept coming back over her, in those waves, and she might easily get lost or run over if she tried to walk. She would have to stay.

So Ione said, 'There's a spare bed that usually has sheets on, in the attic. It's in the room with a green door, and a very long scratch down the paint. It's a very narrow bed, though.'

'That's quite all right,' said Caroline, nose in the air again. 'I am quite small, too, width-wise.'

They said good-night to one another on the first-floor landing. Ione stumbled into her own bedroom, and Caroline pulled herself unsteadily, with the help of the banisters, up the attic stairs in search of a green door with a long scratch down the paintwork.

Both of them were tired to death.

6

The moon-dance around the sundial came to an abrupt halt. Ned had tripped over one of his feet, and fallen over backwards. He lay on the lawn, winded, and stared up at the sky.

'Just look at those *stars*,' he said, in an ecstasy of appreciation. 'Just look at that *moon*.'

Professor Muffet sat down heavily on the other side of the sundial, and lay back on the grass, too. He lay face-up towards the sky, panting. His eyes, like Ned's, were wide open.

'Beautiful,' he agreed. 'Superb.'

He really could see stars, even if he couldn't see the moon. And he could see more stars than Ned could, but of a very different kind.

'Ned,' said Professor Muffet, when he at last had his breathing under control again, and his mind began to grind into action. 'Ned, why won't that fool girl marry you? You're a good lad.'

Deciding that it was probably now safe to approach, Mandy crept up on him, sneaking on her belly across the grass, and he made room under his armpit for her damp nose. Mandy curled up tight and close, to try to get warm again, and went back to sleep.

'No job; no money,' Ned's sad reply floated through the half-light. The moon had gone in again, and the shadow had taken over from the gleam.

Professor Muffet nodded sagely. A wet blade of grass stuck itself to his ear, and he brushed it off.

'But you'll have one and some, one day,' he said.

Ned took time to sort this out. One which? Some what? Ah, yes. One job. Some money. One day. He had a sudden vision of a wallet full of pound notes in his jacket, and lay there intrigued beyond measure.

Meanwhile, Professor Muffet asked, 'What would you like to do most, after you leave next week?'

'Have a baby,' said Ned.

'I beg your pardon?'

'Have Caroline to have a baby,' Ned corrected himself, hastily.

'Why?'

'I *like* babies,' said Ned. He thought it was a silly question and was surprised at the Professor. 'I *want* babies. Lots of them. Cotfuls.'

Professor Muffet thought about all the babies he and Doris used to dream of having. They had hoped for a son, to be called Edward, next.

'What will you call them all?' he asked.

'Caroline,' said Ned.

'Every last one?'

'Every last one.'

'Boys and all?'

'Boys and all.'

'Gracious!'

Mandy woke then, because the damp was seeping through her fur and into her skin. She tried to wriggle her large rump inside Professor Muffet's jacket. He tried, ineffectually, to fight her off. When the battle had at last been resolved in Mandy's favour, Professor Muffet said, 'Ned, I have thought of a solution to your problem.'

Ned jerked himself upright. But his head gave a sickening reel. So he lay down again, gently, to quieten it.

'What?' he asked, weakly.

'Get a job. Earn some money.'

Ned thought about this. It seemed watertight. The vision of the full wallet came over him again. Then he saw the flaw. He said, 'But I'm only interested in doing history.'

'Become an historian, then. Like I am.'

Ned thought about this, too. Then he said, 'I should need to get a very good examination result, though, shouldn't I? And I won't. Because tomorrow afternoon, you and the rest of the tableful of examiners are going to ask me why I wrote what I did in that essay about the Early Sardinian Trade Routes. And so the fact that I still hold these disreputable views on this subject will come to light. And so I shall not get a very good result. And so all will be lost. Nobody on this earth will consider giving me a job as an historian. And so Miss Caroline Hope will reject me for the hundred and oneth and last time, and so we shall never have any baby Carolines in cots.'

His voice trailed away. He had depressed himself.

To cheer himself up, he became fascinated once more in the stars overhead. They seemed to be performing, just for him, a speedy and complicated square-dance.

There was a very long silence. For a while, not even Professor Muffet could think of a way out of this one.

Then, at last, he did.

'Ned,' he said. 'I have thought of a solution to this problem, too.'

'What?' said Ned.

'Dissemble.'

'I beg your pardon?'

'Dissemble. Lie, as it were, not to mince words. Conceal from all the other examiners your disreputable views on the Early Sardinian Trade Routes. Pretend that the essay you wrote – that extraordinary essay – was all a mistake. That it was just the result of a temporary brain-storm, brought on by the strain of your examinations. Pretend to them that you are now a sane man again.'

The more he thought about it, the simpler it all

seemed. He carried on, saying a little more than he really should have done, in his determination to persuade Ned.

'And so you will pass with honours. And then you may even be offered a job at this very University, because Higgins is having to leave to have a long rest, you know. His doctor has ordered a very long rest. And so we need someone else next term to help with all the teaching, while Higgins is away. And if you were to get this job, you would be accepted by Miss Hope. And so you, and she, and all the baby Carolines, will live happily ever after.'

He lay back, delighted with the beauty of it all.

'No,' said Ned.

'Why not?' asked Professor Muffet, irritated.

'There are limits,' said Ned.

Professor Muffet became even more irritated. He was getting cold and he thought that Ned Hump was being very ungracious. He and all the other historians had tried very hard to give Ned a high mark. But Ned's essay on the Early Sardinian Trade Routes had really been atrocious.

It was not as if they minded Ned's disagreeing with them; but if he *did* disagree, he had to give at least one good reason. And all his reasons had been terrible. Professor Muffet remembered one or two of them, and shivered in spite of himself.

On the other hand, all Ned's other essays in the examination had been very good indeed. Which was why he had been able to persusade all the other historians to give Ned this second chance tomorrow.

And now it looked as though Ned was going to throw this second chance away. Ned was just being stubborn and ungrateful, and was acting as though everybody in the world was against him.

So if it hadn't been for the after-effects of the whisky still softening him a little, Professor Muffet would have quite lost his temper with Ned Hump. But as it was, he just said, 'Sad. Sad to see a young man so soon upon the scrap-heap. Flung there to fester by his own stubbornness and stupidity. Sad, oh sad, oh Clio.'

Ned said, 'Sad. Sad to see a man of fame and distinction suggesting to an untried but honest stripling that he should indulge in lies to get himself a job and a stubborn wife, who is probably too nasty to live with for more than a week at a time, anyhow.'

Professor Muffet smiled to himself. He thought that Ned and Caroline would probably fit very well together, married.

Ned was, at this moment, seized with a desire for action. He, too, was getting cold.

He drew up his knees under him. He pulled in his elbows. He gathered himself on to all fours. He pushed hard upwards at the top end, and ended up on two feet. He felt as though he had achieved something great.

He walked round to the other side of the sundial, and held out both hands to find Professor Muffet's. He pulled the Professor to his feet, too.

Mandy rolled out of the jacket sideways, still fast asleep.

'Bed,' said Ned. 'I ought to go home.'

'Impossible,' said Professor Muffet. 'You must sleep here, just for tonight. It would be churlish to throw you out at this time of night, so far from home. You need as much sleep as you can get before tomorrow afternoon; and, in any event, all the buses must long since have ceased to run.'

'Where shall I sleep?' Ned asked. 'I do not wish to sound choosy, but I am not fond of sofas. I am prone to falling off them, and bruising myself rather badly. I think I must have a very tender and sensitive skin.'

Professor Muffet raised his left eyebrow. Then he said, 'I recall that there is a small bed, made-up in case of emergencies such as yourself, in the attic. It lies behind a green door. All the doors up there are green, I would imagine. Most attic doors are. But this one is easily distinguishable, I am told by Mrs. Phipps, on account of a long and deep scratch in the paintwork, which she feels I ought to do something about. Mandy went berserk there, once, whilst Aunt Alice was staying. It was Aunt Alice's fox stole, as I remember, that started all the trouble. I don't blame Mandy in the least. Even *I* could smell that stole several yards away. But anyway, you can sleep there.'

'Where?' said Ned. He was a little confused, and wondered if he was being offered a fox stole to sleep in.

'In the attic,' said Professor Muffet. 'In a bed behind a green door with a scratch. I had thought I made it quite plain.'

He woke his guide-dog up with a loud shout 'Hey, *Mandy*' – and a prod with his foot.

Ned tugged both of them across the lawn and back into the study. While Ned closed and locked the French windows, the Professor bent down to pat his dog good-night.

'Night night,
Sleep tight,
Mind the fleas,
And don't bite,' he told her.

Ned said, 'You look after that dog a lot better than she looks after you.'

Professor Muffet said, in hot defence of his dog, 'She rises to the occasion,' and added, out of honesty, 'on occasions.'

They left the room and parted on the first-floor landing. Professor Muffet stumbled into his own bedroom, and Ned Hump pulled himself unsteadily up the attic stairs, with the help of the banisters, in search of a green door with a long scratch.

Both of them were tired to death.

In the middle of the night, Ione was half-awakened by what seemed to be a series of thumps on the ceiling above her. Her mind was thick with dreaming. She rolled over, thinking vaguely that Caroline must have fallen out of the narrow bed in the attic. But since she had warned Caroline before they parted, and Caroline had been so very up-tight about her own slimness, Ione did not feel in the least bit responsible. She rolled over again, and drifted back, deeper, into her dream.

Soon after he had fallen asleep, Professor Muffet was half-awakened by what seemed to be a series of thumps on the floor of the attic. His mind was thick with the after-effects of whisky, and with dreaming. He rolled over, thinking vaguely that Ned must be prone to falling out of beds as well as off sofas. But there was nothing he could do about Ned's sense of balance, or his tender sensitive skin, and so he did not feel in the least responsible. He rolled over again, and drifted back, deeper, into his dream.

In the middle of the night, Caroline was half-awakened by a cold pressure on her bare shoulder. She rolled over in the narrow attic bed, her mind thick with dreaming. She thought, vaguely, that Mandy must have forced an entry, and be nuzzling up against her. But Caroline decided that she was in no way responsible for Mandy's nocturnal wanderings. She rolled over again, and tried to drift back, deeper, into her dream.

But the coldness came again, on the same shoulder as before.

'Move over,' a voice said. 'Move over. Stop hogging. Move *over*.'

Caroline woke with a start.

She sat bolt upright, clutching the sheet to her bare body.

Ned Hump, dressed in a pair of mauve underpants, a string vest and odd socks, was trying to get into her bed.

Caroline stared. Then she attacked.

'Get out of here *at once*, Ned Hump,' she flared. 'Get *straight* out of my bed and then *straight* out of my room.'

Ned Hump continued trying to shift her over with his elbow.

'Move *over*,' he persisted. He was cold. It had taken him ages to find the green door, and the scratch, and then ages longer to get partly undressed. He was getting colder every moment.

'Move *over*,' he insisted. 'Stop *hogging*. I've been given this bed for the night, you know. So stop hogging and move over, and then perhaps I'll let you stay.'

Caroline lost her temper.

She pushed, as hard as she possibly could, with one foot, without losing either her dignity or her sheet.

Ned Hump fell, heavily, on to the uncarpeted floor.

Caroline said, 'You are the most pushing, illmannered, rude and boorish person in the world. Get out of my bed and my room this *instant*.'

Ned Hump hardly listened. He was tentatively fingering his right thigh. He thought he might well have bruised himself badly by the fall. Then he lost his temper, too.

Ned Hump said, 'You are the most rough, selfish, hoggish and ungenerous woman in the world. Move over *this instant* and let me in that bed.'

Caroline laughed, like a witch.

'You must be *mad*,' she shouted. 'Professor Muffet is right, dead right.' She shifted angrily against the pillows. 'You must be totally *insane* to think that I shall let you into this bed. This is my bed.'

The repetition of the word bed reminded her how tired she was. Her whole body seized up in a yawn, and she only heard the tail end of Ned's next insult. '. . . in the *world*!' she heard him say.

'What?' she said.

Ned floundered around for something even more devastating to say. Finally, he made do with, 'Just you wait till we're married, Caroline Hope. I'll fix you good and proper.'

Caroline was almost asleep. Her violent outburst had exhausted her. But she rallied enough to say, 'You and I shall never ever be married, Ned Hump. Never, ever, ever.'

From way down in the sheets and pillows, she pointed at the door. 'Get out,' she said. 'Get out, get out, get *out*.'

Ned went all cunning.

'I will leave,' he said softly, 'but only, *only* if you promise me faithfully, on your honour, that you *will* marry me; no strings, no fridges, hedges for life and all, within a fortnight.'

'And if I refuse?' The voice came weakly from the pillows.

'Then I shall leap into this bed and attack you.'

Caroline's head reeled.

This could go on all *night*, she thought to herself. This could go on till *morning*. *Nothing* could be worse than this. *Anything*, even fifty years of Ned, would be better than no sleep now.

She collapsed. She gave in entirely.

'I promise,' she said, and fell fast asleep. She could not even keep a grip on her senses long enough to make sure that he kept his promise and left the room.

Made temporarily ecstatic by the success of his ploy, Ned leaned over and kissed her. How odd, he thought to himself, her hair tastes of coconuts.

Then he stood up. He gathered up, from the floor, his shirt, his trousers and his shoes.

At the doorway, he turned back.

'I warn you,' he said. 'I warn you here and now, if you renege, if you back down, if you cheat on me in this, then I shall take an unspeakable revenge upon you. I shall wait. For years, if necessary. I shall wait until your wedding day. The day of the wedding of Miss Caroline Hope to some nice, clean, shaven, respectable, employed Chartered Accountant. A Chartered Accountant with Notions about Roofs Over Heads, and Good Starts in Life, and Little Somethings Put Away In Case Of Rainy Days, and so on and so forth. I shall wait until you are walking, dressed from head to toe in pure white, clutching your lilies, hot-foot from some altar, down some yew-lined, shady church walk. And I shall be there, lurking behind some tombstone. And I shall shout out from behind this tombstone, I shall shout out—' he paused, to think of something perfectly dreadful that he could shout out at her from behind the tombstone, but nothing sprang to mind, so he finished, a little lamely – '—I shall shout out something *perfectly dreadful*, and all the wedding guests will faint from absolute *horror* and *dismay*, and your mother-in-law will *scream* from *sheer shock*, and everyone, just *everyone*, will turn and *stare* at you.'

He left the room.

Caroline, fast asleep, had not heard a single word.

Ned Hump could not find the light-switch in the study, so he could not find the sofa. But he heard, from one corner, Mandy's heavy, drowsy breathing.

Ned and Mandy spent the rest of that night fast asleep together, cuddled up close and warm under the study desk, paw in hand.

7

The first person to wake the next morning was Ione. It was just after five o'clock. The sun was pouring maliciously through her window, lighting up her headache and dazzling her sleep-befuddled brain.

She felt as though she had spent several weeks in a desert. She staggered across her bedroom to the small wash-basin in the corner, and drank four toothmugfuls of minty-tasting water, one after another, straight off. Then she felt her way back into bed, snuggled down and fell fast asleep again.

The second waking, soon after eight, was also Ione's. But this time she felt marvellous – no more thirst, no more headache – just the thought that it was clearly going to be an even more beautiful day than yesterday had been, and there would be four people for breakfast instead of just two. And there was even the hope that Caroline would still be feeling as romantic about Ned as she so obviously had been feeling for at least some of the time, the evening before, and so might agree, at long last, to marry him.

Ione dressed at a frantic speed. She only wore four things, in summery weather, so it hardly took a minute. She did not wash at all. She even left off her sandals in her hurry.

She flew down the stairs, into the sun-soaked hall. On the door-mat lay a note, crumpled from having been pushed in a hurry through the letter box. Ione picked it up and uncrumpled it. It was from Mrs Phipps, and was written in spidery writing on the back of an unpaid gas-bill. The note said:

> *Can't do for you today, dears. Mollie's time has come, and about time too as she's larger than a bus, poor thing, so I am off up there this very moment.*

Ione thrust the note into her jeans pocket, and went through into the kitchen. Here, she stood, in absolute horror and consternation, gazing at the chaos. How *could* she and Caroline have sat in all this mess for so long last night, just giggling and drinking?

Ione set to, determinedly, to clear everything up.

In fact, the mess was not nearly so bad, or so thick, or so encrusted, as it at first sight appeared. And by half past eight, Ione had the kitchen looking almost normal. Everything that moved had been washed up, put away or thrown into the dustbin. Everything that didn't move had been wiped down with a damp dishcloth.

Ione swept the floor, and collected one last dust-panful of scraps, mostly coconut biscuit scraps. She thought that perhaps she ought to mop the floor, as well. She knew it was awfully tacky, because her bare feet stuck to it as she moved around, and at each step she almost had to peel her feet off the tiles. But then she decided that she wouldn't bother, after all, and she went to lay the dining-room table for breakfast, instead.

She pulled another two chairs up to the table, and set out cereals and a toast-rack and sugar and the milk-jug and cutlery and bowls and so forth.

She decided, as she worked, that when each person came down, she might offer to put an egg on to boil; but that any fried-bacon eaters would have to cook their own. She thought she would not be able to bear standing over sizzling bacon in the kitchen, whilst here, out of earshot, everyone else was teasing one another and joking about all the things they had done and said and sung the night before.

When everything was ready, she stopped still for a second. For she could hear, from somewhere upstairs, assorted getting-up noises.

She rushed back into the kitchen, to put out Mandy's food and water, toast the bread and make a large potful of fresh tea.

By the time she returned a few minutes later, with the teapot, only one person had come down and taken a place at the breakfast table, and that was her father. He sat in his usual seat.

Ione put the teapot down on the cork mat, and went back for all the toast. When she returned yet again, he was still the only person sitting there.

Ione sat down in her usual seat.

'Tea?' she asked him.

'Yes, please,' he said, and proffered his stripy blue mug in her direction.

It could, she thought, have been any old day at all.

Professor Muffet drank his tea in silence. He looked most glum. Ione assumed that this was partly because of the drinking of the night before, and partly because he had to spend almost all of a truly beautiful day sitting in a bleak hall, round a table, with a lot of old, equally glum, other historians, examining young people like Ned Hump on their knowledge of Early Sardinian Trade Routes, and the like.

She thought, if she were in his position, she would feel pretty gloomy, too. So she, companionably, kept his silence with him.

After his second piece of toast, Professor Muffet asked his daughter, gravely, 'Ione, do you think that Ned Hump has any sense at all?'

Ione said, promptly and loyally, that she thought he did.

The silence fell between them again. Ione listened for further getting-up sounds through the house, but none were forthcoming.

After his third piece of toast, Professor Muffet

asked, 'Do you think there is any chance whatsoever of his behaving sensibly this afternoon?'

Ione considered. Then she said, dubiously, 'I *think* that I think that there is.'

'I don't,' said the Professor. 'I don't for one moment think that I think that there is.'

He stood up.

'I must go,' he said. 'Or I shall be dreadfully late.' He picked up his jacket from where it hung over the back of his chair. 'Though there would be a consolation in being dreadfully late,' he said. 'I would miss Paul Bisons's performance, which is bound to be abysmal.' Ione dusted off his jacket for him, while he called Mandy in from the kitchen, where she was licking the floor a little cleaner.

Ione passed him Mandy's leading rein, and Professor Muffet strapped it on her. At the front door, with one hand on the latch, and the other restraining Mandy, he kissed his daughter good-bye for the day.

He looked, Ione thought, grey and tired, and very, very depressed. And as he left, he said again, 'I don't for one moment think that I think there is hope. But *if* hope springs, tell Ned that there's a braille copy of Punkle's *Early Sardinian Trade Routes and Their Implications* under the lampstand in the study, and Caroline can read it to him.'

Ione's eyes followed him as he walked down the garden path, dragging his feet a little in the gravel.

She wondered why he was so very fond of Ned

Hump, and so very concerned that Ned should not spoil his second chance.

For the first time ever, it occurred to Ione that her parents might have planned to have more children than just herself. They might well have wanted to have a son as well – a son just like Ned. The more she thought about it, the clearer it all seemed. Of *course* her father would have wanted a son; and he would have loved to have had a son like Ned Hump.

Ione could understand that with no trouble at all. For she would have loved to have had a brother like Ned . . .

Ione made the largest resolution of her life.

She resolved to tell lies, mislead and act – all day if necessary – to get what she wanted.

And what she wanted was that Ned Hump should do as well as he possibly could in his examination that afternoon, so that her father would come home happy again. Ione sat in the sunlight on the bottom stair, and resolved solemnly and silently that not even Ned Hump was going to get the chance to spoil things for himself one single time more.

Ione sat in the sunlight on the bottom stair, and she carefully hatched her plot.

The first part of the plot involved taking Caroline her breakfast in bed, on a tray.

Ione pushed down the handle with her elbow, and kicked the attic door wide open with her foot. She slid inside sideways with the tray, and then set down the tray on the tiny bedside table with as loud a crash as she could manage without breaking anything on it. Caroline still did not stir. So Ione swept the gay, yellow-spotted curtains apart, and the sun streamed in unhampered, waking Caroline far more effectively than the kick on the door and the crashing of the tray had done.

Caroline groaned, and burrowed; but the harsh sunlight seemed to be able to attack her, even through the sheet.

She surrendered to the inevitability of morning, and sat up.

Ione sat on the very end of the bed, on the tattered old patchwork quilt which had been stitched together by Aunt Alice when Uncle Arthur was off at some war, and which was now coming apart into patches again.

'Morning,' said Ione, in her simple voice. 'Super morning. Daddy's gone. Ned's still fast asleep. I'm up, though.'

'So I see,' said Caroline, in her acid voice.

She peered at the tray, and groped for the teacup. 'Is that really *toast*?' she asked, prodding a square, soggy lump that lay dying on a plate. 'It looks centuries old.'

Ione thought privately that, had her plot not been at risk, she could have banged the entire breakfast tray over Caroline's head. She would not even have been scalded. The tea was quite cold, too. But Ione held her tongue.

'The tea is quite cold, too,' said Caroline.

Ione pulled threads out of the quilt. She would have preferred to broach the subject gently, or let it arise naturally out of the conversation. But it did not look as if there was going to *be* much conversation; just a series of insults to her cooking.

Time was, she feared, running short. Ned might get up at any moment, and disappear. There was no time for roundabout openings. She would have to charge almost straight in.

'Does everyone like Ned as much as Daddy and I do?' she said.

'I suppose so.' Caroline leaned back on her pillows, pushing hair from her eyes, and sipped cold tea. 'Most people do. He has one of those faces, I think.'

She was quite pointedly, Ione thought, pretending that the buttered toast no longer existed. However, sacrifices have to be made.

'And does Ned like everyone back?'

'I suppose so,' Caroline yawned. She stretched out, in all directions at once. Ione decided that Caroline was really quite beautiful – all dopey and straggled though she was. Ione also decided that there was no real need to be subtle and roundabout. It was just a waste of time. Caroline was still half-asleep, anyhow.

'It's funny, isn't it,' said Ione, bluntly, 'how some people never seem to get mean, or spiteful or jealous. And Ned seems to be one of those people. I mean, suppose something horrid were to happen to him.

Suppose—' she pretended to think, to come out with the example as though it were the first thing to come into her head, '—suppose somebody else, somebody he didn't like particularly, and thought was dreadful at history, was to be offered this job that is free now that Higgins is having to have a long rest. Would Ned *still* be happy and kind? Is he *really* that nice all through?'

She sat on the end of the bed and waited, casually pulling more threads out of Aunt Alice's quilt. She was hoping desperately that Caroline would take the bait quickly, and yet would not notice that she had done so.

Caroline continued to sip her cold tea. 'I think Ned is fairly easy-going,' she said. 'I mean, that's one of his problems.'

Ione thought of the sundial: 'Seize the present moment, the evening hour is nigh', and the way Ned had read it out loud, just after they met. He had recognised this weakness in himself, too. He had *said* that was another of his problems. So really she would be helping him to be what he knew he ought to be. Lying did unnerve Ione rather, but now she felt quite cheered, and almost justified.

Caroline went on: 'I think he'd remain nice, *whoever* got the job.' She shifted around in the bed. Ione was cramping her feet.

'Is this really tea, or is it coffee?' she asked. 'It tastes a little like both, but not much like either.'

'It's tea,' said Ione, coldly. She was wondering

whether, by furthering Ned's aims to marry Caroline, she was really doing him much of a favour. Caroline could be quite a cow when she tried, Ione thought.

As though to prove this judgement unfair, Caroline smiled warmly. 'He'd be much nicer than *I* would be, anyhow,' she said generously. 'But then, he *is* much nicer than I am.' Ione did not deny this, as she felt courtesy demanded; but she warmed to Caroline again a little. 'And I truly think he'd just be pleased for the person who was given the job.' She giggled. 'Except, of course . . .' At the very thought, she giggled again.

'Except . . .?' repeated Ione, breathless.

Caroline was shaking with amusement. 'Except, of course,' she said, 'if Paul Bisons, or someone like that, who's thick as two planks, and horrid with it, were to get the job. Then, even Ned would go wild.'

She looked up from her tea, expecting Ione to ask her all about Paul Bisons.

But Ione had already rushed from the room. She had the name, and she did not need anything else. Paul Bisons, Paul Bisons, Paul Bisons. She jammed the name into her head on every step of the staircases down.

Caroline shrugged, and finished the coffee-tasting tea. Then she snuggled back down, deliciously, into the bed.

She had no idea how very helpful she had just been.

A very short time after, Ned Hump emerged from

the study, crumpled, grubby and bedraggled. His sleep had been interrupted by the most extraordinary noise, as of elephants cantering down staircases, he thought.

He groped his way down the hall to the kitchen, and found the sink. He splashed cold water all over his face, to waken himself completely. Then he turned back from the sink, his face drenched, and with droplets of water still clinging for dear life to his long eyelashes. His large brown eyes looked huge in his pale, drawn face. Although he would not admit it, even to himself, Ned was chilled by the thought of the afternoon's ordeal.

Ione smiled sweetly at him, and tried to look as though she had been sitting there, with her back straight, calmly peeling vegetables, for hours and hours.

In fact, she had had only a few seconds in which to fill the big plastic bowl from the sink with water, throw in some potatoes from the rack in the larder, and sit herself down in front of the bowl at the table. But Ned did not know that.

And Ione sat there, cool as could be, peeling her potatoes as though she had quite got into the rhythm, and she smiled at him sweetly.

It was a real Caroline smile. Her mind was busy mixing poison, on which she planned to half-choke him.

'Sleep well?' she asked him pleasantly.

'In the end,' he said, and smiled back at her, his

lovely warm smile. His sleep had begun with night-mares about the coming examination. It was only sheer exhaustion that had given him rest at last.

But neither his wan look, nor his friendly smile, deterred Ione in the least from her purpose. She waved a half-peeled potato towards the window, where it caught in a dust-filled stream of sunlight, and said, 'Super day. It's already getting hot.'

'It is,' he said. 'And you shouldn't be stuck in here, peeling spuds. You should be out, lazing on a lawn, chewing daisies and counting butterflies.'

Ione sighed heavily.

'I *have* to stay in,' she said sadly. 'Mrs Phipps isn't coming in today. She sent a note saying Mollie's baby is on the way, and she's had to rush up there to help. So I have to do all the cooking.' She sighed again, even more heavily than before.

'You don't,' said Ned.

He sat opposite, and tugged a lump of bread off the crusty end of the loaf. He began, absently, to chew his way through it.

'You don't have to cook at all. Far too hot. Just wait till everyone is starving, and they don't mind *what* they eat, and then uproot a lettuce, and rush in here for two seconds to open a couple of tins of something. Then go straight outside again.'

Ione said, pathetically, 'It isn't lunch that I have to prepare. It's a proper dinner. For tonight. For a guest. Three courses, and wine, and all that.'

Ned ripped off another lump of bread. That end of

the loaf was beginning to look a little like the moon's surface.

'Who has your father invited for dinner?' he asked, as she had planned he would.

'I don't know, yet,' said Ione. 'It hasn't been decided.'

She waited for him to question this curious statement; but he didn't. For the first time, Ione saw drawbacks in tact like Ned's. So to prompt him, she added, 'I just wish I knew if he's a big potato eater, whoever he is. It's so difficult to know how many to peel, otherwise.'

Ned reached out for a banana. 'It's a he, then, is it?' he said, and added helpfully, 'Usually, you can tell from the person's size. What size are all these men who might, or might not, be invited for dinner?'

Ione carried the bowl of potato peelings around to the sink, behind Ned, and poured the water out. 'It's only a decision between two,' she said. She kept her back to him as the water drained away. She always felt safer, lying, when she had her back to the person to whom she was telling the lies.

She reached out secretly for a little piece of onion she had peeled and placed on the window-sill above the sink.

This is it, she thought to herself. This is it.

'I don't know the size of the other person it could be,' she said slowly. 'I mean, it could be *you* who is invited, in which case I will need to peel lots more.' She paused. 'Or it could be a person called Paul

Bisons.' She paused again, in order to let the name float around the room a little, and not get lost in her sentence. 'In which case I may already have peeled far too many.'

'Why,' said Ned, equally slowly, as he rose to take the bait, 'why should your father choose to invite either Paul Bisons or myself to dinner with him tonight?' Unthinkingly, he placed the banana he had been chewing back on the pile of fruit in the bowl, peeled and half eaten. 'And when,' he continued dangerously, 'am I to know if *I* am the lucky man? Alternatively, when am I to know if Paul Bisons is to be the man who is going to pig all those spuds?'

He finished his questions with real venom in his voice. Ione sang an inward hymn of praise to Caroline, for picking what was so clearly *just* the right name.

'I suppose,' said Ione, pretending to fish in the plughole for small peelings that had got away, but concentrating hard on her lying instead. 'I suppose you will know after your exam this afternoon. You see, Daddy says he ought to invite the man who is asked to take over Higgins's job to dinner tonight. He says it is the custom to invite a new historian to dinner.'

She waited for the explosion.

And it came.

'Paul Bisons?' repeated Ned. 'Paul *Bisons*? The new *historian*? *Paid* to do something he can no more do than sing soprano? Given a *room* in the University in which to write the drivel *he* writes? I can hardly *believe* it.'

Ione plopped all the icing on her lie in one go.

'Daddy says he's very good indeed on the Early Sardinian Trade Routes,' she said.

Ned rose to his feet. He was breathing fast. His face went scarlet with rage.

'I think,' he said, raising his voice, 'I think that your father must have gone just a little *off his head* about these Early Sardinian Trade Routes of his. It seems to be reaching the stage where, if anybody dares to disagree with him about them, that's curtains for them.'

Keeping her back to him, Ione leaned over the sink. She reached out for the small piece of onion. She held it up, as near to her eyes as she could stand, and waited.

'I think,' continued Ned Hump, shouting now at the top of his voice. 'I think that your father is beginning to act a little like *God*, telling everyone what to believe and what not to believe. And only a deity or a fool would wish to invite a brainless cretin like Paul Bisons to take a job within a *thousand miles* of himself, let alone in the same damn *building*. I think,' his voice had risen to a shriek. 'I think that Paul Bisons is the most . . .'

That was when she hit him.

'*Ouch!*' he howled, driven backwards on to the floor, clutching his stomach in a great spasm of pain. For Ione had started her own explosion now. And when Ione decided to explode, she could explode louder and further and better than *ever* Ned Hump could.

She had charged, head lowered, the entire length of the kitchen, and butted Ned in the stomach at full speed. The potato peeler, which she had left in her hand by mistake, had grazed Ned's wrist, and drawn blood, adding a touch of verisimilitude to the performance that Ione would not have dared to aspire to with forethought.

And while Ned sat, winded, on the kitchen floor, clutching at his stomach with one hand, and sucking blood off the other's wrist, Ione ranted at him.

She went wild.

'That's *not fair*,' she shrieked. 'That's not fair *at all*. That's just *so unfair*! You're *crazy*, that's your *problem*. You think that just because you disagree with Daddy, then you're going to do badly in this examination. Well, you're *wrong*, and a *pig*, and *ungrateful*, and *stubborn* and *stupid*! Because Daddy says you don't have to have the same views as he does, and all the other historians have, *at all*. You just have to be able to give one single tiny *reason* for any view that you decide you want to hold. And Daddy says that you *can't*. He says he's been listening to you *all term*, and he says your reasons are *crummy*. And after they read your essay on the Early Sardinian Trade Routes in the examination last month, all the other historians said it was absolutely atrocious, and a *rabbit* couldn't hold views like that without blushing for shame.'

She took a deep breath. Ned was staring at her.

More icing, she thought. More icing.

'So they said to give you one mark, and Daddy said *No*. It was *Daddy* who insisted that you had this second chance. He said you might come to your senses. He told them you were having a little brainstorm from the strain of the exams. He said you were awfully clever really, and you couldn't really believe a word of what you wrote in that dreadful essay. He said you would act sensibly, and think again, and then you might get a really good degree. Because you were only a few marks away, and if it wasn't for that stupid, *stupid* essay, you would have got a really good degree *anyway*.'

Ned Hump stared at her – a little tornado of concern, with tears in her eyes, and a voice that was cracking at the edges. He thought he had never seen anyone lose control so badly.

Ione stared towards Ned Hump. She could not see his face too clearly, because of the onion tears; but she could see him well enough.

More icing, she thought. More icing.

'But Daddy's sick and tired of fighting for you, Ned Hump,' she shouted. 'He says so, and it's true. It shows up, too. Just before he left here this morning, when you hadn't even got *up*, my father was busy trying to find a copy of Punkle's *Early Sardinian Trade Routes and Their Implications*, just in case, *just in case* you decided to act like a sane person for once. He didn't even have time to have any *breakfast* before he left, he was looking so hard. He's probably *starving* now.'

Even Ione felt a little guilty about this wedge of her speech, but she was too far in now to back down. So she went on.

'He's *always* been fond of you, Ned Hump, you stupid, *stupid* idiot, ever since he first began to teach you.'

She broke off, just to keep her head still for a second, so he would be sure to see the tears, before they dried off.

'That's why he calls you a loon,' she went on, when she was quite sure that he had noticed them. 'That's why he calls you the *loon*.' She brushed the onion tears away, so she could see his face properly.

'When I was very young,' she said, her voice soft and quiet now, 'when I was very, very little, he used to call *me* his loon.'

That was enough. That was all the icing there was. Ione stood in the middle of the kitchen and watched, through tear-dampened lashes, as Ned Hump turned ashen-pale.

She watched him thinking, and she knew exactly what he thought. And only when, at last, he climbed to his feet and left the room without a word, did she let her body go all limp.

She dropped down on to a chair and stared into space.

It had been, without a shadow of a doubt, the best performance of her entire life.

From beginning to end, it had been *magnificent*.

A few minutes later, Ned Hump came back into the kitchen. He had stuck an enormous sticking plaster on to his wrist. It was as wide as the scratch was long.

'Where's that Punkle book?' he demanded, with a red face. 'Where *is* it?'

'Daddy put it under the lampstand in the study for you,' said Ione. 'But it's all in braille.'

Ned looked taken aback. Then his face went firm again.

'Go and wake Caroline,' he told her. '*She* can read it to me. Go and wake Caroline.'

Ned went off again, to find the Punkle book, muttering something about Paul Bisons under his breath.

Ione went and woke Caroline.

8

After such a tempestuous start, the rest of that morning seemed strangely quiet and peaceful to Ione.

Ned and Caroline sat together on the bottom verandah step, in the shade from the open French windows. Caroline was reading out, in her soft, chokey voice, all the important bits of the Punkle book, running her fingertips over the braille as fast as she possibly could.

Ned had his arm around her. And as she reached the end of each section, he would nuzzle her ears, for all the world like a friendly horse after sugarlumps. He wanted, more than anything, to hold her hand; but that would have slowed up her reading impossibly, which is why he made do with her ears.

In between the nuzzlings, he was concentrating hard. Read aloud by Caroline, Punkle's views on the Early Sardinian Trade Routes sounded quite sensible. Infinitely more sensible than Ned had ever found them before.

Ione had forsaken her sinkful of potatoes and peelings. She put the potatoes that had been fully peeled into a saucepan of salted water, and she put the ones that she had only half peeled, or hadn't yet started on, back in the green plastic vegetable rack in the larder. She hoped they would dry off without going mouldy first.

There was only one more part of her plot. This was the easiest part of all, and quite the pleasantest. All the big lies were over now.

Ione crept upstairs for her sandals, and then slid as quietly as she could out of the back door, and up the hill to Mollie's house. She wanted to find Mrs Phipps. She needed advice.

She told Mrs Phipps that she wanted to make a splendid, different, surprise, end-of-examination, going-to-get-married, celebration tea for everybody, and make no noise at all while she was doing it, so that no one would guess until the very last moment what she was about.

What should she do?

Mrs Phipps was, at the moment Ione arrived, flustered half to death. She wiped her hands on Mollie's scarlet apron, and tried to think. But thinking was almost impossible. Mollie was very near indeed to having her baby, and yet she was insisting on finishing the game of Scrabble she was playing against her husband, Ted. Mrs Phipps kept telling

Mollie that the game could be finished just as easily with Mollie in bed; but Mollie swore that Ted was not to be trusted for a moment with her pile of letters, and so she refused to obey.

They had, at the very moment Ione arrived, begun to quarrel loudly about whether cocoa was spelt with, or without, an *a* on the end.

Which was why Mrs Phipps was so flustered.

So she tried to think of the simplest solution – the quickest to explain to Ione, that is. She could see, from where she stood upon the doorstep, that the midwife was already on the way, pushing her bicycle towards the bend half-way up Hanger's Hill at a determined pace. It was the bossy midwife, she saw, with a sinking heart. The one who always expected things to be just so. Things were nowhere near just so in Mollie's house.

Mrs Phipps had an inspiration at last.

'Take all the housekeeping money out of the one-and-a-half-pint pudding basin on the third shelf of the larder – that's the pudding basin with the chip on its side – and go down to Waley's in the village and buy a pint of double cream and all the strawberries he has in the shop. And don't you let him sell you yesterday's cream, just because you're young. You take the lid off, right in front of him, and sniff.'

The midwife reached the slight bend that marked the half-way point. Mrs Phipps began to speak so fast that Ione could hardly keep up.

'Mind you go before one, now, because it's early closing day. And whip up the cream a bit with the squiggly tin thing – you'll find that in the spoon drawer – not too much now, not stiff. And take the stumps off all the strawberries and rinse them under the cold tap, and put them in a colander. And at the very last minute, not before, you cut them in half, lengthways, because they go further that way, and you serve them with cream on top in blobs in those knobbly glass dishes, and go easy with the sugar. Use castor sugar and go easy with it.'

'Won't a whole pint of double cream and all the strawberries in Waley's cost an awful lot?' Ione asked, appalled at the thought of such extravagance. After all, they would only be four for tea.

'Of course it will,' came the reply, promptly enough. 'That's why it's special.'

But Mrs Phipps had assumed that, with all Ione had listed to be celebrated, there must be at least a dozen people coming.

Then she saw Ione's worried look.

'Now don't you fret,' she told Ione. She was a motherly soul, except with Mollie, who wouldn't be mothered. 'Your father will never guess. I'll feed you both on kippers and lentil soup for a fortnight, to make up.'

Relieved, Ione rushed down the path to the gate, almost colliding with the midwife's bicycle. Just as she was apologising, Mrs Phipps called to her again.

'If it's *really* special,' she said. 'Go down the cellar,

and mind all those dreadful rotten steps or you'll fall and hurt yourself, and get out some of the white wine, and bung that in the fridge, too, to keep cool.'

She had not been Professor Muffet's daily help for years for nothing.

'Gosh,' said Ione. She thought she really had started something.

Mollie yelled then, good and loud and long. In fact, it was because she had just looked up cocoa in the dictionary, and it *did* have an *a* on the end, but Ted stubbornly refused to look, and believe her.

But Mrs Phipps and the midwife did not know that, and they shooed Ione out of the garden altogether.

Ione ambled through her errands. It was getting hotter, fast.

She found the housekeeping money in the pudding basin, though it wasn't on the third shelf at all, unless you were counting upwards from the floor, which was, Ione thought, daft. She walked down to Waley's, and bought the cream and the strawberries. She trusted to Mr Waley's honesty that it was fresh cream. She would never have dared to open the carton in front of him and all his other customers, and sniff.

She whipped up the cream with the squiggly tin thing, not too much. She took the stumps off the strawberries, and ran the tap over them, and then put everything in the fridge.

After that, she washed all the knobbly glass bowls and all the small spoons.

Lastly, she opened the cellar door, and peered down into the dark. It was here that her courage failed her completely. For there was no electric light in the cellar.

She wondered if she dared interrupt Ned's working, to ask for his help. She crept along the hall, and into the study, and peered out through the French windows.

The Punkle book was lying forgotten on the lawn, its edges curling upwards in the sun's heat, and Ned and Caroline were kissing.

Ione walked out.

'Ned,' she said, after a polite little cough, 'are you afraid of cobwebs and spiders and the dark and all that?'

Caroline spoke first.

'I bet he's scared of spiders,' she said. 'It's more than likely. He's scared of me, and I only have *two* arms.'

She attacked Ned with her two arms, and they fell together off the bottom step and on to the lawn.

Ione waited patiently for them to unravel. Then she said, 'Ned, would you please go down into the cellar for me?'

Ned shook some blades of grass and his wife-to-be off his shoulders, and said, 'Lady, lead on,' chivalrously to Ione.

Ione showed him the cellar door, and lit him a

candle. Ned stepped down two of the creaking, planky steps into the gloom.

'Before the darkness swallows me entirely,' he said, 'perhaps never to yield my fair body up to you again, would you be so good as to tell me what you are sending me down here for? Or is it merely attempted murder, like this morning?' He held out his plastered wrist for her to feel guilty.

Ione giggled.

'Wine,' she told him. 'White wine.'

'Wine,' he repeated. 'White wine.' He looked up at her sternly. 'What *sort* of white wine?'

She considered. Her secret was at risk. And since she had been lying to him all morning, one more little one couldn't matter much.

So she said, 'I'm not sure. I've forgotten what Daddy called it. But I remember that it's the same sort as we had one day when we had strawberries and cream at Aunt Alice's house.'

Ione really was a superb liar, when she put her mind to it.

'Oh, *hock*,' said Ned, and disappeared, apart from a few mild flickerings of his candle, into the cellar deeps.

Ione waited, on tenterhooks, at the top of the steps. A short while later, from below, Ned sent up a loud and echoing shout. 'How many bottles?'

Ione counted up people. Four people, with luck. For it did seem as if Caroline was going to stay all day.

'Eight,' she said.

'*Eight?*'

'Eight.'

'Eight.'

At that moment, Ned was attacked by a ferocious spider, and so was distracted from asking any more difficult questions. He brought up the bottles in two journeys, and Ione stacked them, lying on their sides, in the fridge. She kept the fridge door half shut, as she did so, so that Ned could not see the strawberries or the cream that were already inside.

Before putting the last bottle in, she looked at its label.

'It doesn't *say* hock,' she accused him, suspiciously.

She wasn't sure exactly what it *did* say, because everything on the label was in German; but she was sure that it didn't say hock.

Ned Hump leaned against the table and took up another banana from the fruit bowl. He seemed to be addicted to bananas.

'That's one of the great mysteries of wine,' he informed her. 'That is why I stick to cider. It's cheaper, and you know where you are, or rather, you know what it is, because it tells you, on the label, in large, red English letters.'

He added over his shoulder, with his mouth full of banana, as he returned to Caroline, 'Also, you can keep cider in sensible places, like in the larder, or under your bed. You don't feel obliged to keep it in a dark cellar, with no light, where, in their turn, giant belligerent spiders feel obliged to attack you each time you feel like a quick swig.'

His voice trailed away.

Ione giggled. She loved the way he talked.

She went off to the study, to find some glasses. They would probably need washing, too, she thought. Judging by the smears all over the knobbly bowls, Mrs Phipps obviously had her blind spots as a daily help.

Just before two, Ned came back into the kitchen. He looked quite smart.

'I have stolen one of your father's shirts for the day,' he said. 'And a tie. This shirt must be far too large for him, since it almost fits me.' He ran a finger around the back of his neck, to loosen it a little. 'Almost,' he repeated, uneasily.

'And now I have come to ask you to make me a sandwich. Since I appear to be living here at present, it seems only fair that I should be fed, at least for today.'

Ione began to butter him some rolls and fill them up with large slabs of cheese. She knew that cheese was nourishing. As fast as she could fill the rolls, Ned ate them, talking all the while between mouthfuls.

'I am leaving this house now,' he told her. 'I have listened to as much of Punkle's *Early Sardinian Trade Routes and Their Implications* as I can stomach, and now I am going to go for a very long walk in order to clear my head. Kindly keep my wife-to-be from following me. She only distracts.'

'Is Caroline really going to marry you?' asked Ione. 'Really and truly?'

'I think I have beaten her into submission,' said Ned, complacently. 'I think she has bored herself into weakness with all those refusals. I think the worm has, at long last, turned.'

He waved a bridge roll at her.

'I shall not come back here between my walk and the exam,' he said. 'So whether or not I return to this house ever again will depend on how that exam goes. In the event of its going badly, I shall take drastic action, and you will find my body bleeding gently in some nearby ditch, a few days hence.' He took another mouthful. 'In the interests of history,' he added, 'I shall leave a trail of evidence to convince the police that I was, in fact, murdered by Paul Bisons. I trust you will employ your time, after the initial bout of grief, getting up petitions to send to the Home Secretary for the re-introduction of the death penalty.' He looked at her face. It was a little blank. 'Hanging,' he said. 'Hanging.'

She grinned.

'And if it all goes all right?' she said.

'In that case, I shall return soon after four o'clock with your father, a broad smile, a flagon of cider in my arms and a small golden ring in my pocket for my beloved to wear as soon as she can be organised into a Registry Office, or something.'

'It's early closing day,' said Ione.

Ned left, clutching three bridge rolls and another banana.

Soon after, Ione drifted out into the garden. The sun was very high, and very powerful. Even the grass looked a little weak from the heat.

Caroline was lying on her stomach on the lawn, picking petals off a daisy.

'He loves me, he loves me not, he loves me, he loves me not, he loves me, he loves me not,' she was singing softly to herself.

'Of *course* he loves you,' said Ione, as she sat down beside her. 'That's why he came here yesterday. That's why he was trespassing in our summer-house in the first place. That's why he's so thin, from not eating enough for fear you'd never marry him. That's why I invited him in, and gave him all the chocolate biscuits. And they're awfully fattening.'

Caroline picked another daisy. 'He'll do well this afternoon, he won't do well, he'll do well, he won't do well,' she sang instead, shredding this daisy, too.

'Of *course* he'll do well,' said Ione. '*You* know he will; *I* know he will; *Daddy* knows he will; even *Ned* knows he will, now. Daddy says he's one of the brightest young men he's ever taught.'

Caroline rooted around for another daisy. She had to stretch to get at it. All her hair fell into her eyes. The sun caught it, and it shone spangles.

She began ripping this daisy apart. 'He'll get a

job, he won't get a job, he'll get a job, he won't get a job,' she sang, petal by shredded petal.

'Of *course* he'll get a job,' said Ione. 'Daddy says they need someone else desperately, to take over from poor old Higgins while he has his rest; and it's far too late to ask anyone else now. And Ned will be very good at teaching, so they'll probably keep him on, even after Higgins comes back. Ned's a really good teacher. He's taught me an awful lot.'

Caroline rolled over on to her back, and shut her eyes against the harsh, half-past-two sun.

'Ione,' she said. 'I only hope that there is another man in the world as nice as Ned Hump, for you to fall in love with some day.'

Ione thought this was a lovely thing to say.

She swallowed hard.

Ione thought that Caroline was so very different now, and yet not really different at all. It was just that this side of her had never really showed up much before. This gentle, not-so-irritable side.

It occurred to Ione that always, in the beginning, she had seen Caroline when she was Miss Hope, who was always working or pouring out the tea, and so she had been in her efficient mood.

And then, when she had seen her with Ned, Caroline had probably been irritable because she loved him so much, and was dreadfully worried about him and his future. After all, even Ione's father got irritable with Ned Hump some of the time, and he wasn't planning on marrying him.

She thought that Caroline was probably really nice all through, like Ned, after all. And she was glad about that. Ione wanted the very best for Ned. She had done ever since she had first met him.

Ever since. Ever since? It was only yesterday. Only yesterday that she had met him, and not even, yet, the same time as yesterday.

At this time yesterday, she hadn't even *met* Ned Hump. She could hardly believe it. She had met him just as the sun sank into the hedge, if you were sitting on the summer-house floor. Not quite a whole day ago. And yet she felt as if she had known Ned Hump for years and years and years.

She felt full up, and sad, and as though, if something didn't happen quickly, she would burst into tears.

But something did happen.

Mrs Phipps called over the hedge, as she sailed by on Ted's bicycle, 'Mollie's had a *girl*, and now they're squabbling about what to call it, I mean her, and . . .'

Her voice was whisked away by the draught created by the speed of the bicycle.

Ione lay back again. She rubbed the sadness tears back into her eyes.

'How super for Mollie,' she said.

Beside her, Caroline smiled at the sun, eyes tightly closed.

'How super for *me*,' she said softly. 'And once, when he met your mother, how super for your father.

And soon, not long from now, how super for *you*.'

And Ione smiled up at the sun, too, red and yellow through her closed eyelids. And warm, safe and warm.

'How super for me,' she repeated. 'Soon, not long from now, how super for *me*.'

9

All that afternoon they lay, Caroline and Ione, dead to the world, lulled by the sun's warmth, sleeping.

From time to time, Caroline would giggle softly inside her dream. Sometimes, Ione's fingertips would scrabble against the turf, unknowingly.

They slept, side by side on the yellowing grass, as though they might never, ever wake.

But they were awakened, in the end, by Mandy.

Just before five, she bounded across the daisies, released from her leading rein at the garden gate by Professor Muffet. She flew over the lawn, placed two rude and heavy paws on Caroline's stomach, and reached over to lick Ione's ear.

Both of them sat up, blinking against the sun and the sleep and the drowsiness of the whole afternoon. From the wickerwork gate in the hedge came the sound of voices, and a small procession of about a dozen people, mostly men, began to straggle untidily into the garden, droning on about this and that, the voices getting clearer and clearer across the closer sound of Mandy's friendly snuffles.

'Lord,' said Ione. 'People.'

'Lots,' agreed Caroline. 'They must be all the examiners, come back for a cup of tea.' She sat up, suddenly, more straight, as she realised what this meant. 'Can you see Ned?' she demanded anxiously of Ione. 'Is he there? Is he with them? Can you *see* him?'

Ione could. He was somewhere towards the back of the straggle, not yet through the gate. He was staggering under the weight of an enormous glass flagon of cider. His teeth were bared in an horrific grin, and from between his clenched teeth there was suspended a brown paper bag.

Spotting them, he speeded up to overtake the others, who were much too deep in their conversations to notice even his frantic elbowings and shoves. He finally made his way through, and over the grass to them. He towered above Caroline, clutching the cider flagon to Professor Muffet's shirt. He opened his mouth, and the brown paper bag, soggy at one end, and with tooth marks, fell into Caroline's lap.

'Take it,' he told her. 'It's for you.'

She peered into the bag and up-ended it. Into her palm dropped a shining brass curtain ring. It glistened as bravely as it could, only being brass, in the sunlight.

'Oh, Ned,' said Caroline. 'It's lovely.' And she burst into tears.

She slipped the curtain ring on to her wedding finger. It fell off again at once. It was far too large.

'Never mind,' she said, licking tears of happiness off her flushed cheeks. 'Doesn't matter.' She stuck the curtain ring firmly and proudly on to her thumb. It fitted perfectly. 'I *love* thumb rings,' she said.

'I think you'll have to,' said Ned. 'They'd never alter it. It only cost five pence. I had to buy five. I threw the other four away. It's not a real ring, you see. I did so want to get you a real, gold, people's ring,' he added wistfully. 'But it was early closing day.'

His eyes *dared* Ione to tell him she had told him so. So she didn't.

'Only Woolworth's would let me in to buy *anything*,' he went on, in explanation. 'And only then because there were three ladies in there, stock-taking, and I banged on the door so loudly and for so long.'

'Never mind,' said Caroline again. 'Doesn't matter. I *love* thumb rings.'

She gazed straight up at him with the look of moonstruck adoration that Ione had so often seen Ned use on her when she was looking the other way.

Ione decided it was time to be tactful again. So she slid away, leaving them together, and threaded her way through the historians and the conversations, in search of her father.

She found him by the shrubbery, talking to an

incredibly old man with hands gnarled like bits of tree roots. He wore a deaf-aid, spectacles and a large white tropical sun-hat.

'Ione,' said Professor Muffet to his daughter, 'I would like you to meet the Emeritus Professor of Ancient History.' Then he bent down and whispered in her ear. 'Emeritus means retired. And he's deaf, so you have to shout.' Then he shouted, 'Bill, meet my daughter, Ione.'

Ione wondered if she ought to curtsey. He looked so unbelievably old. He might even be expecting it of her.

The Emeritus Professor of Ancient History peered at Ione.

'Spittin' image of her mother,' he said, after a lengthy inspection. 'Same eyes. Lovely eyes. *Always* liked Doris's eyes,' he added wistfully.

Ione's father looked pleased. Ione, unaccountably, felt pleased, too. She had never before particularly wanted to look like her mother. All the photos that there were of Doris Muffet made her out such a frump. But Ione quite liked the idea of sharing her mother's eyes.

To cover her embarrassment at the compliment, though, she asked, 'Did Ned get all his answers right?'

Her father winced at the question. 'It isn't quite as *simple* as that, at Ned's stage,' he began to explain. But Ione could not wait till the end of an explanation, so she turned to the Emeritus Professor of

Ancient History. 'Did he?' she asked him. 'Did Ned get his answers right?'

'Wouldn't know,' came the reply. 'Wasn't there. I only met everybody outside Woolworth's, during the smash-and-grab, as we thought at the time. Thought I'd come along for a spot of tea, if there *is* any . . .' he said, looking around hopefully.

In desperation, Ione caught the arm of a perfect stranger. 'Please tell me,' she said, 'how Ned Hump did.'

The man said, without even thinking her question odd, 'A splendid performance, really splendid. Especially considering that earlier essay. Couldn't have done better myself on the Early Sardinian Trade Routes, and I've been into them quite deeply, you know.'

He turned back, and took up his former conversation.

Professor Muffet laid an arm on his daughter's shoulder.

'There's no need to *fret*,' he told her. 'Everything worked out beautifully. We practically offered him the job on the spot, except, of course, that that would never have done and we had to wait till afterwards.'

'Did he say yes?'

'Of course he said yes,' said Professor Muffet. 'It would have been most churlish of him not to, after all our efforts.'

Ione smiled to herself. And mine, she thought. And mine.

Professor Muffet had turned back to the Emeritus Professor of Ancient History. 'We had a few doubts about Hump at one time, you know,' he said. 'He was acting most strangely.'

'Like outside Woolworth's?' asked the Emeritus Professor of Ancient History, with interest, still half believing that Ned had been forcibly restrained from an all out smash-and-grab.

'Not exactly,' said Ione's father. 'But he's quite well now, thank God. And it's only a fill-in job, till Higgins has had his long rest – that's why we didn't have to advertise – so if he goes odd again . . .' There was no threat in his voice though. He didn't believe Ned would.

'And if he doesn't go odd, can you keep him on after Higgins gets back?' asked Ione.

Professor Muffet hummed and hahed and we'll see'd; but he meant yes.

'So glad,' said the Emeritus Professor of Ancient History. 'Though of course, he's not my period, and anyhow, I'm retired. But he seems a nice lad. Apart from his turns.' He made a half turn, to assure himself that Ned was not in the immediate vicinity, and said to Ione, 'He says some very strange things, you know. I asked him, outside Woolworth's, how he hurt his wrist. I thought his answer might be important evidence against him, when he came to trial. I think he probably cut it in some other smash-and-grab attack, earlier in the day. Can you imagine what he said? He said that a lady had tried to peel him to death.'

He scratched his off-white hair, under his bright, white sun-hat. 'Odd thing to say, don't you think?' he said. 'Seems a nice lad, though.' He scratched his head again, and turned to Professor Muffet. 'You'll have to watch this passion of his for cider,' he told him. 'That sort of thing can break up a lot of good research. Is he a Somerset lad, do you think?'

His eyes strayed round in search of Ned, to see if he looked like a Somerset lad; but something in the shrubbery caught his attention instead. He stayed only long enough to add, 'And a bit of an embarrassment outside Woolworth's, don't you think? After all, they were closed. I don't believe the curtain-ring tale for one moment, myself. After all, he threw them all away, a few yards down the street.'

He shambled off towards the shrubbery. 'Seems a nice lad, though,' he let fall, charitably, over his shoulder.

Ione stopped jumping around.

'Daddy,' she said. 'Mollie has had a baby girl, and I have surprises in the fridge.'

Ione's father smiled to himself. He had met Mrs Phipps in the village, and Mrs Phipps was incapable of keeping a secret. But Ione's father could take a secret to the grave with him, so he did not tell Ione that he had met Mrs Phipps. However, he did allow himself to say, 'Secrets in the fridge? How splendid. And a baby girl? How wonderful. But what I would have liked *most* in the world, on an afternoon like this one, is . . .' He paused, interminably. 'Let me think.

116

What I would have liked most in the world on an afternoon like this one is strawberries and cream; and to wash it all down, let me think again . . .' He tried quickly to think of what Ione might have come across first, rooting around in the cellar in the dark.

'Hock?' asked Ione, as casual as she could be in her excitement.

'Why, yes,' said Professor Muffet, astounded, and not for the first time, either, by his daughter. 'Hock would have been just the thing.'

As Ione sped away, he said to the Emeritus Professor of Ancient History, 'You're right, Bill. She *is* the spitting image of her mother.'

But since the Emeritus Professor of Ancient History was already deep in the thickest part of the shrubbery, his comment fell on no ears at all, let alone deaf ones.

Ned steered Caroline out of the flock of muttering historians and led her to a patch of quiet on the edge of the lawn.

'When shall we two meet again?' he asked her. 'In thunder, lightning or in rain? Or have you time for a quick wedding on Saturday morning?'

In answer, she kissed him. Not for the first time that day, but certainly for the longest.

In the kitchen, Ione was desperately slicing strawberries in half, lengthwise, to make them go further, and dropping them into the knobbly glass bowls. She ladled cream on top in thick splodges, and wedged a spoon down the side of each bowl. She forgot the castor sugar entirely in her impatience, which was probably a good thing, since she was so jittery that she would almost certainly have poured on too much.

She rushed out, with the first trayful, on to the lawn, and offered bowls to all the nearest people. Then she spotted Ned.

'Ned,' she cried. '*Ned!* The *bottles!*'

Ned rose to the occasion like a well-trained butler. He stopped kissing Caroline at once, and ran for the kitchen, where he dug a corkscrew from the spoon drawer, and pulled the bottles, one after another, from the fridge.

Ione rushed in after him.

'Tea-towel,' said Ned.

She passed him one.

'Glasses,' he ordered.

She held them up, one by one, as he filled them almost to the brim.

'Tray,' he said.

She set as many as she could on the tray.

'Move,' he told her. 'Mingle and give. Return post-haste.'

She moved as fast as she could without spilling a drop of the wine.

'And send in Caroline,' Ned shouted after her. 'It's about time she was some use. She can go round with one of these bottles, and fill up people's glasses.'

Then he leaned against the fridge, and wondered how on earth Ione had *known* he would be offered a job, and they would all come back for tea, and strawberries and cream in such vast quantities would be called for, and eight bottles, at least, would be drunk.

He never did find out that the answer was simple. On her tenterhooks, that morning, when she tried to calculate the number of bottles Ned should bring up from the cellar, Ione had multiplied bottles by people, instead of dividing.

A quarter of an hour later, Ione stood with the last two bowls of strawberries on the edge of the shrubbery. Everyone in sight was already eating, or had already refused, a bowlful. To whom should she give the only two second helpings? It was a hard decision for someone who saw strawberries as rarely as Ione did.

Just then, the Emeritus Professor of Ancient History battered his way, like a large jungle beast, out of the shrubbery. Bits of twig were sticking to his clothing, and his hat was awry.

Ione handed him one of the two knobbly bowls. As he took it from her, and peered down to see what it was, his eyes lit up.

'Just the thing,' he said, appreciatively. 'Just the very thing.' He squeezed her free hand with his free hand. '*Just* like your mother, you are, dear,' he said. '*Just* like her.'

Ione walked away on air. She ate every last one of

the strawberries in the last bowlful, without feeling an ounce of guilt.

Everybody became quite happy very quickly, and most friendly. When the hock had all been drunk, some people stopped drinking altogether, and some shared in Ned's cider.

Ione thought that everybody was wonderful. Everyone who spoke to *her* first said something kind or flattering; and every one *she* spoke to first, interrupted her to tell her how much they were enjoying themselves, or how good the strawberries had been.

Ione worked her way around the guests to her father again.

'You're marvellous,' he told her. 'You're wonderful.' He was feeling rather euphoric.

'What shall we do,' she asked him, 'when Caroline has married Ned, and they have gone away on honeymoon?' She twisted her fingers round. 'My braille reading is still so *slow*,' she added.

Professor Muffet tried to hack a sensible thought out of his wine-soaked brain.

'We shall have to phone the Agency,' he decided. 'And ask them to send me another Caroline for a few weeks. When do you think that she and Ned will marry?'

'Tomorrow, I should think,' said Ione. 'From the way they have been carrying on today.'

'Oh, my dear me,' said Professor Muffet. 'Take me

to the phone at once. Why is that damn dog *never* around when I need her?'

'Because you always let her go off,' said Ione. 'That's why they gave you the rein.'

She took his hand firmly, and he trailed along beside her to the study.

After Professor Muffet had at last remembered the Agency's full name, Ione found its number in the book. She dialled, since Professor Muffet appeared to be a little too unsteady to attempt the feat. Though he usually could, by filling up dialling holes with his fingers, to mark his place, till he reached the hole he wanted.

The pleasant lady who had sent them Caroline answered, and Professor Muffet explained his problem to her. And it *was* a problem, she reminded him sternly. Sighted girls who knew braille were awfully hard to find, she told him. They did not grow on trees. She said it would take at least three weeks to find him a replacement, and possibly even longer. Most of the girls she could think of were sunning themselves on Spanish beaches, just at the moment. Oh, yes. It would be at least three weeks.

'Oh, well,' said Professor Muffet. 'Caroline will be back by then. And she can work while she's having babies, can't she?'

The pleasant lady at the other end of the line gave a rather loud gulp.

'Up to a point,' she said at last. 'Up to a fairly well-defined point.'

'*Exactly*,' said Professor Muffet, and he thanked her again, and rang off. He was, though he would never have admitted it, a little relieved. He tended to be wary of any strange woman – especially any young one whose job was to organise him. That was why Miss Hope had been called Miss Hope for so long, and not Caroline.

'Well,' he said to his daughter. 'How long do you think they will be away?'

Ione considered. Then she said, 'I expect that they'll plan to go away for two weeks, and then they'll take another week on top of that to organise themselves back home again. Ned is that sort anyway, and Caroline seems to have lost her efficient mood altogether.'

'Three weeks,' mused her father. 'Three whole weeks.' Then he beamed. 'Three *weeks*,' he said, elatedly. '*Three whole weeks.*'

'So?' said Ione. She was beyond understanding.

'Don't you see?' he cried, amazed that she didn't. 'Don't you *see*? Three whole *weeks*. Can't work. Can't do a thing, really. No point. If I fill up the tape-recorder, and the tic-tac thing, and everything else with work, and then Caroline comes back from her honeymoon and sees it all piled up waiting for her, she'll leave me. She'll half-kill me. So we might as well take a holiday ourselves.'

'A *holiday*? You and *me*?'

'And Mandy, of course.'

'A *real* holiday? Away from here? Me too? At the *sea*?' Ione was beside herself.

'At the sea, if you like. Anywhere. I don't mind. Not fussy at all, as long as we're miles from Aunt Alice.' He beamed again. 'Haven't had a holiday for *years*, have we? Not for years and years and *years*.'

Ione hugged herself. Then she hugged him. Then they went back on to the lawn, to the remains of their dwindling party, hand in hand. Ione was so excited that she let her father tread on an empty strawberry bowl that someone had left on the grass, near the sundial. It broke with a crunching sound, under his foot.

'Was it a knobbly one?' asked Professor Muffet. 'I never did care for those knobbly ones.'

The Emeritus Professor of Ancient History bore down upon them. 'I say,' he said. 'Splendid *hamamelis mollis* you've got there, in the shrubbery, near that egg-cosy thing. Mind if I take a cutting back for the wife?'

'Splendid what?' asked Ione.

The Emeritus Professor of Ancient History stared at Ione. He was amazed by her ignorance. What, he asked himself, *did* they teach them, nowadays? '*Hamamelis mollis*,' he repeated. 'Chinese witch-hazel. *Hamamelis mollis*.'

Ione's father made an enormous gesture, sending the large white tropical sun-hat flying.

'Take the whole thing,' he said, expansively. 'Uproot it. Carry it off. Take it home. We don't need it any longer. We're going to have a holiday.' He squeezed his daughter's hand, tightly.

'Couldn't possibly,' said the Emeritus Professor of Ancient History. 'Far too big. Can't think what you mean.'

But his comment fell on no ears at all. Ione and her father had moved off.

Just towards six, just as the sun was nearing the hedge, Ione felt her head begin to swim.

Her father was deep in a boring discussion with someone she didn't know. They were arguing about food riots in Berkshire.

So she detached her hand from his, without his noticing, and slid off quietly, to find somewhere where she could be alone, and sort herself out.

On the way across the lawn she noticed Caroline in the study, holding the phone to her ear. Ione waved. Caroline waved back, phone and all.

'I'm ringing our parents,' she called out. 'Will you and your father be free on Monday morning? *Please* say you will. We shall be getting married. They can't fit us in on Saturday.'

'Oh, yes,' said Ione. Her voice sounded almost as chokey as Caroline's. 'Oh, yes. Yes, please.'

She hurried off to the solitude of the summerhouse, before she disgraced herself in front of the few remaining guests, with her tears.

10

On the summer-house floor, yesterday's diamonds were back, just as before.

It might almost have been as though they, and Ione, had never been gone; and as though nothing whatever had happened between then and now.

Ione sat, cross-legged, on the floor, tracing patterns with her fingertips on the cool, grey flagstones. She was thinking.

She was thinking about Caroline, and Ned, and her father, and Mandy, and Mrs Phipps, and Mollie and Ted and the baby girl, and the Emeritus Professor of Ancient History, and of all that had happened in the last twenty-four hours.

And she was thinking about the holiday that was going to happen after the wedding on Monday.

She thought, now that the sudden bout of sobbing that had attacked her a few minutes before was quite over, that she was probably perfectly, perfectly happy.

The diamond reflections where she sat were, once again, long and elegant. Those by the far side were, once again, squat and ugly. The sun was nearly down into the hedge. The noises from the lawn died away entirely as the last guest said good-bye. And Ione sat on, in a daze, watching the last diamonds fade. It was just like yesterday.

And then she heard his voice behind her, just as before. Her heart gave such a jump that she missed hearing what he said; but she knew it was him. And she also knew that he must have seen her coming in here, and followed her from the lawn; but with his usual tact, he had waited until her crying fit was all over before he had spoken.

So she turned round to smile at him. He stood there, tall and thin, with his green jacket dangling from his fingers behind his back, picking up all the dust from the doorpost that it hadn't already picked up the day before.

'*Plus ça change* . . .' he said.

'What does that mean?' she asked him.

She thought it might well be one of the very last things that she ever learned from Ned Hump, who had taught her so much; so she wanted to get it exactly right.

'It's a French proverb,' he told her. 'It means: the more things change, the more they stay the same.'

She thought about it. Then she said, 'That's not true, though. That's not true at all.'

'No,' he said. 'I never thought it was, either.'

He moved across, and dropped down in front of her. He lifted her chin with two fingers, and she forgot about the tearstains on her face.

'If it wasn't for you,' he told her, 'if it wasn't for you, I wouldn't have been able to marry Caroline, and I wouldn't have been given the job. I would have spoiled everything for myself, as usual, if it wasn't for you.'

She shook her face free, gently.

'Loon,' she said.

She knew, if he went on, she would begin to cry all over again, and harder.

'Maybe,' he said, understanding. 'But I can *thank* you, can't I?'

And he gave her a kiss on the cheek. His long, droopy moustache tickled.

Then he turned and left her summer-house, as silently as he had come into it. And he had come, as she knew, just to see her.

'Loon,' she said softly again, as the last diamond folded up into itself and faded away.

'Soon,' she comforted herself, softly, 'soon, not long from now, how super for *me*.'

The Other
Darker Ned

'Mope. That's all she ever seems to do now-adays. She hardly ever speaks. She just sits down at the bottom of the garden inside that silly giant egg cosy of a summer-house of hers.'

Ione is young, passionate and idealistic and easily bored in the long summer holidays with no-one for company but her blind father. But that was before she met Ned, cheerful, well-fed and unconcerned with his scatty new bride. The perfect threesome.

Anne Fine

The Stone Menagerie

Every Sunday Ally goes with his parents to visit his shadow-like Auntie Chloe in a mental hospital. Every Sunday Ally gets angry, thinking the visits a total waste of time. Until, one day, he sees the girl who has planted her own name in the mysterious, tangly land on the other side of the lake . . .

Anne Fine, winner of the Smarties Prize for *Bill's New Frock* and the Guardian Fiction Prize and Carnegie Medal for *Goggle-Eyes*, is much praised for her wit, ingenuity and 'sense of depth under playful surfaces, a light touch which can reveal the poignancy in the happiest relationship.'

'This is another excellent novel from a remarkable writer.'
Peter Hollindale, *British Book News*

A Selected List of Fiction from Mammoth

While every effort is made to keep prices low, it is sometimes necessary to increase prices at short notice. Mandarin Paperbacks reserves the right to show new retail prices on covers which may differ from those previously advertised in the text or elsewhere.

The prices shown below were correct at the time of going to press.

☐	7497 0978 2	**Trial of Anna Cotman**	Vivien Alcock	£2.50
☐	7497 0712 7	**Under the Enchanter**	Nina Beachcroft	£2.50
☐	7497 0106 4	**Rescuing Gloria**	Gillian Cross	£2.50
☐	7497 0035 1	**The Animals of Farthing Wood**	Colin Dann	£3.50
☐	7497 0613 9	**The Cuckoo Plant**	Adam Ford	£3.50
☐	7497 0443 8	**Fast From the Gate**	Michael Hardcastle	£1.99
☐	7497 0136 6	**I Am David**	Anne Holm	£2.99
☐	7497 0295 8	**First Term**	Mary Hooper	£2.99
☐	7497 0033 5	**Lives of Christopher Chant**	Diana Wynne Jones	£2.99
☐	7497 0601 5	**The Revenge of Samuel Stokes**	Penelope Lively	£2.99
☐	7497 0344 X	**The Haunting**	Margaret Mahy	£2.99
☐	7497 0537 X	**Why The Whales Came**	Michael Morpurgo	£2.99
☐	7497 0831 X	**The Snow Spider**	Jenny Nimmo	£2.99
☐	7497 0992 8	**My Friend Flicka**	Mary O'Hara	£2.99
☐	7497 0525 6	**The Message**	Judith O'Neill	£2.99
☐	7497 0410 1	**Space Demons**	Gillian Rubinstein	£2.50
☐	7497 0151 X	**The Flawed Glass**	Ian Strachan	£2.99

All these books are available at your bookshop or newsagent, or can be ordered direct from the publisher. Just tick the titles you want and fill in the form below.

Mandarin Paperbacks, Cash Sales Department, PO Box 11, Falmouth, Cornwall TR10 9EN.

Please send cheque or postal order, no currency, for purchase price quoted and allow the following for postage and packing:

UK including BFPO — £1.00 for the first book, 50p for the second and 30p for each additional book ordered to a maximum charge of £3.00.

Overseas including Eire — £2 for the first book, £1.00 for the second and 50p for each additional book thereafter.

NAME (Block letters) ....

ADDRESS ....

....

☐ I enclose my remittance for ....

☐ I wish to pay by Access/Visa Card Number

Expiry Date